*Treasure
for
Treasure*

Books by Justin Scott

Many Happy Returns
Treasure for Treasure

TREASURE FOR TREASURE

Justin Scott

David McKay Company, Inc.
Ives Washburn, Inc.
New York

Treasure for Treasure

Designed by R. R. Duchi

LIBRARY OF CONGRESS CATALOG CARD NUMBER: 73-93030

MANUFACTURED IN THE UNITED STATES OF AMERICA

ISBN: 0-679-50444-3

For Don

Treasure
for
Treasure

Chapter 1

It looked like a rock, but it wasn't a rock so I picked it up for a better look, because one thing I know is rocks. Not that I'm a geologist or anything, but I've shoveled maybe a trillion rocks in my time and I'm only twenty-five. When you've been a sandhog for seven years, you handle a lot more rocks than the name would imply.

Anyway, I picked up the rock, but before I could examine it Rifkins, the foreman, yelled, "Creegan."

That's me, Dick Creegan, so I yelled, "What?"

"Stop screwing around and get back to work."

I told the rock something clever about Rifkins and slipped it into my pocket. The bald-headed foreman shouldered his way up to me and asked if I cared to repeat myself. I said I hadn't said anything, picked up my shovel and went back to scooping muck out of the shield into the battleship.

I'll explain that right now for anybody who isn't a sandhog. There are less than a thousand of us in the whole country. A shield is a tremendous steel cylinder in which we dig tunnels under rivers and bays. It's the cutting edge of the tunnel and moves forward like the jaws of an earthworm, swallowing the mud it doesn't push aside.

Rifkins lurched off to terrorize somebody else and I kept shoveling. Then it happened again. I dumped some muck into the battleship and there was another one of those rocks that wasn't a rock. I grabbed it and knelt down by the battleship to see if there were any more of the things.

I was going to tell you about the battleship. It's a strange name for a very ordinary little hopper into which we shovel what we're shoveling. When it fills up we send it down rails to the airlock at the beginning of the tunnel.

I pawed through the muck looking for more rocks that weren't rocks. Rifkins bellowed and I leaped for my shovel. This time he yelled something about my playing with mud pies. I tried to form an answer that wouldn't make me lose face, either physically or mentally, but the quitting bell rang and Rifkins suddenly had more important things to do.

We dropped our tools and headed for the decompression chamber. The tunnel was about half done. It ran from the west shore of Welfare Island to the middle of the East River. When we reached the other side we would find ourselves on Manhattan Island, provided the engineers knew what they were doing. Actually, the tunnel I was working in was the third part of a railway passage that would connect the borough of Queens with the borough of Manhattan. The second part was being cut through Welfare Island by hard-rock miners. The first already ran under the other half of the East River, from Welfare Island's east shore to Queens.

We walked toward a tremendous bulkhead at the beginning of our tunnel. On the other side of the bulkhead the air pressure was normal. Here it was about five pounds per square inch higher. In between was the airlock–decompression chamber.

As we trooped in, Rifkins counted heads carefully. Twice. Then he nodded to Burke, who swung the steel door shut and wheeled the lock tight. He manipulated the valve that would bring us back to normal in about an hour. The rest of us dropped onto the wooden benches.

I collapsed. It was the end of our second three-hour shift. At times like that you're almost grateful for the decompression period. You're so damned tired that if you were able to go straight out you'd fall on your face in the street. For fifteen minutes I sat slumped forward. Finally I was sufficiently rested to be bored. I looked around but nobody looked like they felt like talking so I pulled my book from my pocket and read until Burke opened the airlock door.

The next crew was already down. They exchanged greetings and filed into the airlock to begin their shift.

The elevator took us the couple of hundred feet to the surface and deposited us right outside the hoghouse, a kind of locker room, shower, bedroom and office. I dropped my clothes on the floor, fell into a shower, very hot, emerged steaming and clean, toweled off and climbed into street clothes, which were, for me, dungarees and a heavy black turtleneck. I stepped into my boots and kicked my work clothes into my locker. It was late November and cold out. I put on the old sheepskin coat my old man gave me before he died and started to close the locker.

The rocks.

I fished into the work shirt pocket, found them, dropped them in the sheep, closed the locker and headed out the door, hoping to find Jeannie on the other side.

Chapter 2

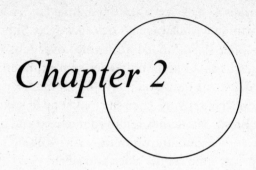

Jeannie and Howard were waiting at the gate.

I said, "Hi, Jeannie. Hi, Howard."

Jeannie kissed me lightly on the cheek and Howard granted me a surly nod. I kissed Jeannie on the mouth and stepped back for a better look. She wore her tremendously thick, brown hair long and straight. Little bangs were swept to each side of her forehead, complimenting her high cheek bones and forming her face into a sort of oval diamond. Her eyes were blue and her mouth was wide and I still wondered what she saw in me.

"I thought you might like a ride," she said.

I thanked her, said I would and asked her what she was doing about dinner. She asked me if I'd like to have some at her place. I said yes and we strolled toward her car. Howard got in the back and I sat up front with Jeannie.

She drove off Welfare Island onto Vernon Boulevard in Queens, over the Fifty-ninth Street Bridge and down Second Avenue. I still wasn't used to all the people staring. Pedestrians and drivers alike did double takes when they saw Jeannie's Rollswagen. Or Volksroyce. Shortly before I met her she'd landed a fat voice-over job. She spoke the words in a one-minute television commercial and they paid her six thousand bucks for her time. So she bought a new Volkswagen. Then she took it up to a body shop in the Bronx where they removed the front end and replaced it with a miniature replica of a Rolls Royce front, and painted the results black and silver.

It looked exactly like a Volkswagen with a Rolls Royce nose. It also looked like a pig with a bad cold. And people stared. Just like they stared when they saw Jeannie sashaying down the street with Howard. I think she wanted it that way.

"How'd it go today?" I asked.

"Unbelievable."

"Find anything?"

"I read for a part."

"What kind?"

"A bisexual dwarf chambermaid."

"Aren't you a bit tall?"

"I thought so. My agent said we'd work it out."

"Do you think you'll get it?"

"No. They said I looked too young." She cut off a Con Ed van and turned with a grin. "Think I can still do an ingenue?"

"No," I said. "Sorry."

"I didn't think so," she said lightly. Jeannie was twenty-nine and looked it in the best way. She referred to herself as a working actress. What she meant was she made a living by playing small parts in Broadway and Off Broadway productions and doing occasional commercials. When she was desperate she'd do some modeling. She got by, but it demanded a lot of hustling around from call to call. The big part in the sky hadn't yet come her way.

At the end of Second Avenue she turned right onto Houston.

"How about you?" she asked.

"I found something strange," I said. "Look." I pulled the rocks that weren't rocks out of my sheep and held them in front of her. She glanced down from the road and crinkled her eyes.

"Rocks?"

"I don't think so. Look." I scraped them together. Their surfaces flaked away, dropping wet dust to the floor of the car.

"Hey, Hog. Watch the dirt."

"Sorry." I brushed off the seat and put the rocks that weren't rocks back in my pocket. We were crossing Sixth Avenue and Jeannie grabbed her sonic box off the dashboard and pressed the button. Her building's garage door slid open.

She had a nice apartment on the fifth floor, big living room, two small bedrooms and a decent-sized kitchen. It seemed like more room than she and Howard needed, but she'd gotten the place several years ago before rents in the city had become ridiculous.

I dropped onto her tremendous suede couch. A moment later she returned with a couple of vodka martinis and sat next to me. Howard appropriated his usual chair on the other side of the room. "Cheers," said Jeannie. "Hungry?"

7

"Cheers," said I. "Not really. Could you give me a glass of water?"

"Help yourself."

I found glass and water in the kitchen, and a small knife. Returning to the living room, I placed the glass on the coffee table and dropped in my rocks that weren't rocks.

"What?" asked Jeannie.

"Maybe the water'll soak the outside loose," I replied.

Jeannie took a sip and looked at me. "What's with you and those rocks, Hog?"

"There's something about them. I've never seen anything like it."

The water was turning thinly brown. "They look like a couple of balls of mud," said Jeannie.

"But they're not. You notice how they're almost exactly the same size. And shape. And also, they're not round all the way around."

"What are you talking about?"

"It's softening," I said. "See what I mean? It's flat."

Jeannie seemed intrigued now also. "What is it?"

I took the knife and poked at the muddy circle. It was about an inch in diameter. With the knife point I made several indentations, twisting the blade each time to scrape more of the mud off. Jeannie was leaning forward to see what I was doing. Her hair lay over my arm and I could smell its perfume. I glanced up at her. In concentration her face was more beautiful than ever. I slipped and stuck the knife into my fingertip.

"Ouch, dammit." I shook the finger.

"Oh, Hog," said Jeannie. She forced my finger into the water, wiped away the mud and looked at the cut. Then she took my finger in her mouth and sucked sharply. The pain went away immediately. She took my finger out and looked at it. "Better?" she asked and licked it with her pointed tongue. I said it was and told her that if she didn't stop arousing my finger I would leap on her and make love to her right there and then in her living room.

"Great idea," she replied, lying back on the couch and smiling. I dropped the flat thing back in the glass of water and lay next to her. I looked up once but Howard had fallen asleep.

Chapter 3

Good smells were coming from the kitchen. I had covered Jeannie's coffee table with newspaper and was in the process of scraping the rest of the mud from what was definitely some kind of flat circle. Finally, when it seemed the knife would be of no more help, I went into the kitchen. Jeannie was deftly turning some fried bananas. In the next pan chicken was sizzling. She leaned back against me.

"How you doing?"

"Good," I said. "Have you got some steel wool?"

She pointed with a dripping spatula.

The steel wool cut through the mud quickly. What remained seemed to be metal. There were highs and lows on the flat surface, as if it had been carved. I buffed some more.

"Jeannie," I called. "Come here."

"Gold?" she asked.

"I think so." I held the polished surface under a lamp. The high parts were all shining brightly.

"It's a coin," Jeannie said.

"I think you're right."

"What's on the other side?"

"I haven't done it yet."

"Do it after we eat. I'm starving."

I laid the coin next to my plate and headed for the bathroom to wash my hands. When I returned Jeannie was just placing Howard's dish before him in the kitchen. He attacked it with more vigor than he'd expended all day. Jeannie and I watched him for a moment, then made our way to the dining table at one end of the living room.

We ate silently, mostly because I wasn't doing anything with my mouth but filling it. Only after I'd cleared the table while Jeannie poured coffee and sat back down did I have another look at the metal lump.

We decided it was indeed a coin. More polishing revealed a cross, letters—undecipherable—and numbers, equally vague. A few minutes later the reverse side shone as brightly, showing more lettering and a shield.

"You found a gold coin," said Jeannie.

"Where do you suppose it came from?" I asked.

"Seeing as how you're digging a tunnel under the East River," Jeannie said, "I suppose it came from the East River."

"Brilliant," said I. "And how do you suppose it got there?"

"Somebody must have dropped it."

"But the tunnel is at least thirty feet below the river bottom," I said.

"Maybe they dropped it a long time ago and it's been drifting down through the mud."

"But I found two of them. It seems strange that if somebody dropped two coins they'd both end up so close together after all those years. Doesn't it?"

Jeannie frowned, digesting that. Then she said, "Of course if they'd dropped a lot of them that would make it more likely, wouldn't it?"

"And I just found two? Yes. I suppose so."

"Too bad you didn't find more," Jeannie said. "You'd be rich."

"Sure."

"If it's gold it must be worth something."

Jeannie took the coin, leaned back on the couch where we were sitting, and moved it slowly in the lamplight. It cast sparkles that bounced from the walls and ceiling. Howard lifted his head. His little eyes followed them around. His ears pricked forward.

"What would you do if you were rich?" Jeannie asked.

"Me?" I thought about it for a few seconds. "I'd love it," I said. "Fantastic idea. Yeah. I'd like that very much."

"But what would you do?"

"Spend it, of course."

"On what?" she said with a smile. Every now and then I'd get this feeling that she was a hell of a lot older than me. I mean she was about four years older. But sometimes she'd slip into a thirty-year-old woman role and I'd begin to feel like a little kid.

"I don't know what," I said. "A good car. Maybe a house. I never had a house. Might be nice to settle down in one spot for more than a few months at a time. I'm liking New York. It's becoming home."

"So it would really change your life?"

"It would give me a chance to find something else to do. Though I don't know what."

"Become an actor," Jeannie said. "We'll do a two-man show. Tour the country." She grinned.

"I have toured the country," I said. "More times than the Gideon Bible man."

"So we'll tour the world."

"I've dug tunnels in Egypt, France and Indonesia. And when I was a kid I followed my old man when he dug tunnels in Japan and India."

Jeannie grinned some more. "We'll tour Brooklyn and Queens."

"Can't we just stay in Manhattan?"

"Okay. Manhattan it is."

"But I'm not an actor."

Jeannie sat up, grabbed my head and pulled me down. "I'll take care of you," she whispered. "Stick with me, kid."

I kissed her and said, "That's a nice-sounding offer. Let me think about it." Jeannie let me go and sat back up. "You're not the type," she said lightly.

"Neither are you."

"I know." She fell silent and stared across the room at Howard. He roused himself from his stupor, pulled himself to his feet and stumbled over to lay his head on her lap. "Hello, Howard," she said quietly. I looked at her. There was a different tone in her voice. She looked into Howard's eyes. But when she spoke she was talking to me.

"Hog?"

"What?"

"My agent is working something on the Coast."

"A part?"

"In a television series."

"Congratulations."

"I don't have it yet. It's just in the first stages. But if I got it I'd have to go out there."

"Oh." I was surprised and a little hurt that she hadn't mentioned it to me.

Several weeks before, I'd been wandering around the Village when I came across a tiny theatre showing *A Streetcar Named Desire.* I'd recently read the play, reading being a habit my old man had taught me, and one which he'd picked up from a trade unionist in England when he was younger. I'd never seen the play performed, so I gave it a try.

The moment the curtain went up I was transfixed. First by the beauty of the woman who played Blanche and then by the way she played her. It was so stunning that I couldn't even get up between acts and when it was over I sat in a daze while the rest of the audience filed out.

After a while Blanche emerged from behind the curtain and hurried up the single aisle in a sweater and jeans with an expensive-looking suede coat over one arm. I grabbed a discarded program, found her name, jumped up in front of her and spewed compliments.

Jeannie had looked at me quizzically, but with none of the coolness such an admiring assault might have drawn.

"I'm glad you liked it," she said in a strong voice that was somewhat different from the one she'd used for Blanche. I got ahold of myself enough to stop babbling and said, "Could you join me for a drink?"

Her quizzical look turned speculative for a moment, then doubtful. She smiled politely. "You're very kind, but I don't usually drink with strangers."

"You can depend on my kindness," I said.

Jeannie laughed. "Always?"

"Always."

She smiled and said she would and we found a bar and talked until the place closed. I walked her home, around the corner, and we made plans for dinner the next night. We'd spent three or four nights a week together ever since, and the only snag in our relationship was an actor-turned-playwright named Loren.

I never quite understood their relationship and she'd made it clear early on she wasn't about to explain it. They were friends. He was writing a play she liked. Supposedly there was a big part in it for her. Her life was unscheduled day to day and when we did get together it was always by her initiative. Tonight, it seemed, Loren was busy writing or hunting backers and I was the lucky one who shared her company. I don't mean to say that she played the two of us off each other. In fact, she had been careful to keep us apart. It wasn't the best situation as far as I was concerned, but I liked her too much to risk losing her by demanding something she wouldn't give.

"Oh is right," said Jeannie. "I really don't know what to do."

I was trying to think of what I would do if she suddenly went to Hollywood. "When will you know?" I asked.

"A few weeks. Maybe less. Then I'll have to go right out. In fact, I might have to fly out to see people in the next few days."

"What are your chances of getting it?"

"Pretty good," she said, with little enthusiasm.

"You don't sound happy."

She held Howard's head with both hands and turned it

back and forth. Still looking in his eyes she said, "I just feel I'm so close to making it here in New York. On the stage. Settling for television seems like resignation. Do you know what I mean?" Her eyes swept up from Howard and met mine.

"I don't know the differences," I replied slowly. "I do know I'd be happier if you stayed here."

She laughed. "I guess I would be too. But a chance like this doesn't come every day and I haven't made it here yet, big, and I might never. I'm good. So are a lot of people. Hundreds of them. It's such a luck business." She stared at me blankly for several minutes. Then, moodily, she said, "I'd miss you, Hog."

Chapter 4

We started the shift, the next day, by moving the shield forward eighteen inches. First we positioned the hydraulic jacks against the last ring of the heading. Then with one of us on each jack, and Rifkins calling out the orders, the shield was shoved forward, inch by inch. It moved easily at first, but then Kosinski, who was on the lower left, complained of resistance.

While the rest of us stood by, Rifkins inspected Kosinski's jack. It seemed to be functioning properly, so he told Kosinski to up the power. The rest of us kept an eye on the edges of the advancing face to make sure Kosinski didn't slew the shield out of line. After some hesitation, and an inspection for leaking air, Kosinski's jack pushed his quadrant of the shield into position.

We kept pushing until the shield was far enough forward to permit the iron men to begin assembling the next ring. While they did that, I approached the forward doors to empty the mud.

I started on the lower left. The third door revealed lumps in the mud. I grabbed one, thinking I'd found another coin. But as I tapped the mud away, the interior crumbled to nothing. I inspected another lump. Again it happened, and this time I noticed that the crumbly interior seemed to be made of wood.

A cool pricking moved up my neck and under the hair at the back of my head. I caught Rifkins's eye and waved him over. He came swiftly, probably because my face looked bad.

"What's wrong?"

"Look." I handed him the lump and picked up a few more. He stared at it for a moment. "Wood?" he asked.

"I think so."

"How the hell did it get here?"

"I don't know," I said. "What should we do?"

"Keep your eyes open. I'm going to try another door."

He meant I should watch for any signs of a blow, because the shield had moved into uncertain ground, and the mud might suddenly be changing to water. Carefully, he braced himself against another door and opened it a crack. When nothing came spewing out, he opened wider, grabbed some of the contents, and slammed it shut.

"More wood?" I asked.

"Looks like it." He seemed worried. His eyes flickered over the curved ceiling.

"Hold everything," he yelled. Everyone stopped what they were doing and looked at Rifkins. "Anybody hear a blow?" he called.

Men shook their heads.

"See any water?" Everyone inspected the walls around them, paying particular attention to the rear edge of the shield. With none of the tools going, a semblance of silence fell over the heading. Men cocked their ears for the sound of escaping air and looked at each other. No one was smiling.

The phone rang. The guy nearest it answered, then held it out for Rifkins, who was already reaching.

He listened for a moment. Then he said, "Keep the air up," and dropped the phone into its cradle.

"They've spotted bubbles up top. They're dumping clay. We're leaking a little. Shut all the doors. Anybody not putting up iron get sandbags ready and watch for a blow. You guys on the iron get it up fast. Burke, get any crap in the way out of the way."

Rifkins glanced around. "Kosinski."

The giant nodded gravely.

"You're lock tender." For a second everyone stared at Kosinski. Rifkins was putting his strongest man on the door of the airlock, in case it had to be shut against the water. The lock tender has to decide when to shut the door, which means he might have to shut it before everyone is through.

"Move!" yelled Rifkins. We moved. I stacked sand-bags and bales of hay kept in the heading for the purpose of plugging holes. The iron men slammed their curved rings into place as fast as they could, enlisting some of the muck shovelers to bolt them in.

The danger was that the exposed part of the heading between the completed walls and the back of the pushed-forward shield would not hold the air pressure until that eighteen-inch circle could be filled in with steel and grout. Suddenly I heard hissing air. Before I could

19

move Rifkins shouldered past, heaving a sandbag at a little pucker in the mud. As he let the bag go and swung his arms back down, I handed him another sandbag. He threw that one too, but it just disappeared into the pucker with a slurping roar. I heaved the next one myself and felt the pressure suck the thing out of my hands. More men moved in, hurling sandbags and hay bales at the widening hole. The air rushed past us, like wind. The hole opened farther, to about three feet in diameter. I could feel my ears popping with the reducing pressure.

For the first time I was really scared. That hole wasn't getting any smaller and within seconds it might get too big for the compressors to keep up with it. Blindly I threw another bale. Two feet from the hole it was yanked out of my grasp.

Rifkins threw another sandbag and watched it disappear instantly. The heading had blown.

"OUT!" he yelled. "GET OUT!"

The iron men dashed down the tunnel to the distant airlock. Burke followed them. I was right behind him, running into a powerful torrent of air rushing out the hole and up into the river. It must have been blowing a geyser forty feet above the water.

When I was halfway to the airlock, the roar of escaping air ceased suddenly. For a second there was silence. Then a new sound, thicker and harsher, filled the tunnel. I looked back. Water poured in, in a four-foot stream. Within a second it was around my ankles. Another second and it reached my knees. I ran like hell, pumping my feet above the water and leaping in fits and starts as it grabbed my thighs.

Ahead, the iron men were into the lock. Burke leaped the bulkhead and joined them. Kosinski leaned his weight against the half-closed door, bellowing to run. I snapped a look over my shoulder. A tidal wave was rushing down the tunnel. Rifkins, the last man in the heading, a few feet behind me, must have seen the horror on my face because he turned to look back. It threw him off balance and he stumbled and pitched forward into the water. For an instant I hesitated. The entrance to the airlock was still ten feet ahead. Rifkins thrashed around behind me. Then the rushing stream carried his struggling body next to me. Running toward the airlock, I looped a hand into his belt and slung him to his feet with strength I hadn't known I possessed.

A second later I dove through the lock door. Kosinski reached out and heaved Rifkins after me with one hand, then threw his weight against the door. Water spilled over the bulkhead and began filling the lock. Burke piled in behind Kosinski, adding his weight against the door. The tidal wave, four feet above the rest of the stream, was almost on top of us. I shoved with my hands and shoulders against Burke and Kosinski. Three iron men shoved me. Slowly, the door closed tighter.

The water spurting through the narrowing crack turned to a fine sheet of spray like a piece of glass. The spray grew finer, but broadened as the water suddenly thrust harder, forcing us back a few inches. Kosinski gasped and gathered himself like spring steel.

"Heave," he muttered, shoving his body into the door. Those of us behind him flattened his body against the steel. The spray narrowed again. Then the tidal wave slammed into the door, rocking it open six inches. Water rose in the cramped chamber. The lights flickered. Someone yelled something that turned into a scream of terror, which seemed to galvanize us to push harder. For the third time the gushing water narrowed. The spray grew finer and finer and disappeared so slowly and gently, like a collapsed spider web, that we shoved and cursed for several seconds after the door was entirely shut.

Kosinski shrugged us off his back, spun the lock wheels, then sagged against the metal. His face was ashen. I looked at the others. You could smell the fear. My hands trembled and suddenly I was cold.

Rifkins darted to the air controls to rebuild the pressure in the lock. We'd left the pressure we'd been in too quickly, though the pressure had really left us. Now it had to be returned to the former levels immediately and then slowly released or we'd all get the bends.

It got warmer as the pressure increased. I stopped shivering and gradually the trembling went away. What wouldn't go away was the memory of the wall of water that had marched down the heading tossing steel hoppers like ping pong balls and twisting a catwalk into a bundle of crumpled pipe.

Rifkins nudged me. "Thanks for picking me up."

I felt scary laughter rise in my throat. "My pleasure," I choked.

"Anybody hurt?" Rifkins asked, looking around. One of the iron men had twisted his ankle. Another had a long shallow gash from his wrist to his elbow. We'd been lucky. Kosinski removed the first aid kit from its locker and bandaged the iron worker's arm.

"Well," asked Burke, "do we go back in or call it a day?"

It wasn't a particularly good joke, but everyone laughed as they settled down on the benches, which were nearly submerged, and waited for the decompression.

Rifkins picked up the phone and told the people up top what had happened.

A bunch of doctors and male nurses were waiting outside the airlock. They threw blankets around us and hurried us up the elevator and into the hoghouse. When you come out of pressure your pores are wide open, leaving you susceptible to pneumonia. Coming out of the tunnel drenched by the flood waters only made things worse. The doctors made sure everyone took first hot then cool showers, something all of us knew to do anyway. Then they patched up the cuts and bruises and left us.

I got my hands on some coffee and stood by the front window watching the construction disaster ritual of the arrival of the brass and the press.

Long black limousines roared over the gravel drive and crunched to sliding halts in front of the office. Shirt-sleeved managers raced out and opened doors for grey-suited company brass, who sprang from their cars with grave excitement in their faces.

A lackey stood nearby with a stack of hardhats, and as each car emptied its cargo, he handed them to the site manager, who handed them to the new arrivals, who put them on over twenty-dollar haircuts and horn-rimmed glasses. Patting their new toys into place, they marched briskly to the elevator at the top of the shaft, peered in as if they'd see something important, and hurried into the office where it was warm and another lackey had hot coffee and danishes waiting. If the guy was really important, one of the chief engineers would pour him a shot of rye in the back room.

The press arrived and clamored their way into the office, where the guys in grey suits told them what it was like to get caught in a blow. Later, a sandhog might have a few drinks in a nearby bar with one of the better reporters, who'd write it like it was and then finish the story with a pile of nonsense about hardhats, short hair and patriotism.

The office door swung open and the hardhatted brass made a beeline for the hoghouse.

"Here they come," I called over my shoulder.

"Good work, men," Burke mimicked in a loud squeak. A moment later the president of the Metropolitan Tunnel Company walked in. His name was Doorman. He was short and shiny and talked like a guy who sold swampland to pensioners.

"Good work, men," he squeaked. "Glad you all got out."

"Us too," said Burke.

The president nodded vigorously. "I'm sure you are, son." He advanced on Burke and grasped his hand, moving alongside with an arm over his shoulder. One of the vice presidents pointed a newspaper photographer at them. The guy said, "Hold it," and his flash blinded everybody.

"One more?" asked the president.

"Yes sir," said the photographer and shot another picture.

The president dropped Burke's hand like a snake. "All right, boys," he said to the reporters. "We've got business to discuss, if you'll excuse us." The press were already heading back to the office, with the look of men hunting a drink. One of them said, "Thank you, Mr. President," as he hurried after his cohorts.

Doorman babbled for a few minutes about safety and bravery and left. The project manager made us wait around for another hour to make sure none of us would keel over with the bends. They finally let us go, with warnings to make sure we had compressed-air worker cards to identify us as sandhogs, so that if someone found us lying in the street they could ship us back to the hospital lock at the site. It was just late morning. Getting the tunnel sealed and pumped out wasn't our problem, so Burke and Kosinski and Rifkins and I piled into Rifkins's car and headed for Charley's, a bar in Long Island City.

Already the memory of the blow was fading, as if the mind knew when it had had enough and would keep it out of action until it could be handled better.

Chapter 5

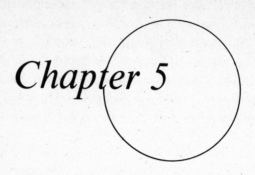

When you work for a living and something, like a
    blowout, disrupts the routine, you feel very special
heading for a warm bar on a cold day at noon. It's
different from after work, or on Sunday.

We walked into Charley's looking like we owned the
place. I'm a hair under six feet tall and weigh one-ninety,
but I look rather slight next to Rifkins, Burke or
Kosinski.

Charley, who owns the place, reached for his billy
before he recognized us. Satisfied we'd been there
before, he left it in easy reach and asked for our orders.
Everyone asked for beer. And everyone, except me,
asked for rye to go with it. I try to keep away from
whiskey before lunch.

Actually, Charley had little to fear from us. Rifkins
usually confined his shouts and threats to the job. He got

on well with Kosinski, who never said anything. Burke was fairly boisterous in an unconscious way. I am meek and mild-mannered.

But by two o'clock I had developed a headache and knew I had to get out of there for some air. Rather than get into a big argument about not staying and drinking, I slipped out when no one was looking and went for a walk. I was thinking about Jeannie and how upset we both were when she said she might go to Los Angeles. So when I passed a phone booth, I dug out some change and gave her a call. She wasn't home, her answering machine told me, so I told the machine to tell her I liked her very much and hung up. Then I stood in the phone booth awhile looking over the two gold coins I'd found the day before. My headache told me I didn't want to go back to Charley's. I thought of going to my own place, but that wasn't very appealing because it was in a rooming house in Long Island City that was owned by the same old woman who seemed to own every rooming house that ever went into business within walking distance of a sandhog tunnel under construction.

I thumbed through a tattered Yellow Pages until I found the heading for numismatists. I was rather proud I had remembered the word. The Yellow Pages listing for numismatists, however, directed me to "Coin Dealers, Supls., Etc." There I found a bunch of listings in the West Forties in Manhattan. Checking out my coins had to be better than my rooming house, so I got out of the phone booth and into a cab, which I had take me to the corner of Sixth Avenue and West Forty-seventh Street. I walked toward Seventh Avenue looking into the windows of several stores that claimed to deal in coins. On the basis of nothing in particular I entered one. The guy behind the glass counter was dealing with another customer so I sort of walked around and looked.

Glass shelves and counters held displays of mostly new-looking coins. They were wrapped in plastic and most seemed to be sold in sets. In among the coins were magnifying glasses for sale plus coin displayers, polishing and cleaning kits, coin magazines and coin newspapers.

The guy and the customer were concluding their transaction. As I listened I had the funny feeling I'd heard it all someplace before. I once spent the night drinking with a pair of divers who'd been called in to shut a watertight door that hadn't held. It was interesting at first, amusing after a while, and deadly in the end. Before long they'd forgotten I was there. These two coin nuts were going at it the same way. Happy to have found each other and able to communicate as they could with none other.

When the customer finally left I took out one of my gold coins and held it before the guy's face as he asked me if he could help. He looked about thirty, had slicked-down curly hair, short sideburns, a strong nose, black-rimmed glasses, a leather penholder in his white shirt pocket and a crisp voice. He looked like a guy who might come around to fix your television. When he got through with it it would work.

He looked at the coin, started to ask me what it was, apparently changed his mind, reached down and came up with a magnifying glass, and asked, "May I?"

I dropped the coin into his outstretched palm.

For several minutes he stared at it through his glass. His face stayed still as his eyes flickered and darted.

Abruptly he lowered his glass and laid the coin on the counter top.

"Very nice," he said, with a quick smile. "Very nice."

"What is it?" I asked. As soon as I said it I knew I'd made a mistake. A millisecond of surprise dislocated his features. But by the time he answered he had them all back together.

"It is," he said, "an eighteenth-century Spanish doubloon. Where did you get it?"

"Is it very rare?" I asked.

"Not particularly. Where did you get it?"

"Is it particularly valuable?" I asked, picking it up.

"Not particularly . . . I mean the market fluctuates up and down—moves around. You know how these things are." He smiled carefully. "May I ask where you got it?" he asked.

"How's the market right now?" I asked.

"Oh. Down a bit. I suppose you got it in Florida or someplace like that?"

"Uhhh," I said because I didn't like the way he kept asking.

"Well, if you want to sell it," he said, "I'll give you, oh, ten bucks. Wait. It's in nice shape. Fifteen."

If I was reading this guy right, I figured the coin must be worth about sixty. I had no intention of selling it, however, but I decided to watch him work up. He took my silence for negotiation, it seemed, because he came back a moment later with an offer for twenty-five. At that point I figured my coin must have been worth about eighty.

"I'm sorry," I said, "but I don't think I'm ready to sell."

"Thirty."

"I was thinking of making a necklace for my girl friend out of it."

"You'll destroy its value if you put a hole in it," he cautioned.

"Maybe I'll just work a ring around the edge if I can. Anyway, I've got another if I blow it."

"Another?" he asked. Before I could answer, the door opened behind me. The guy behind the counter stiffened slightly and moved a bit to one side. I turned around to see what was going on.

"I'm here for my quarter," said the largest Times Square Thug I'd ever seen. He was wearing a newly stolen windbreaker over some old clothes. While he didn't point a switchblade at me or the guy who owned the store, he made it quite clear he had one in his pocket. The handle peeped out boldly. I turned back around to look at the coin guy. To my surprise he was completely in charge of himself. When I saw why, I stood very, very still and got ready to go for the floor. His hand was resting an inch above a gun clipped behind the counter.

The coin guy spoke in his crisp voice. "The door is behind you, man. Get on the other side of it."

The Times Square Thug was stunned. From the looks of him, the last person who'd addressed him in that manner had been his mother's pediatrician. He shook his head disbelievingly.

"What you say, man?"

"Out! Now!" said the coin dealer. "While you still can."

Something in his voice was completely credible. The Times Square Thug gave me a puzzled glance and shuffled out the door. When I turned around the coin dealer was standing back in front of me again. The guy had an amazing way of talking. I knew that the Times Square Thug couldn't possibly have seen his gun, but he'd backed off anyway.

"I have a permit," he said offhandedly. "Now, you were about to settle for sixty-five dollars for the two coins, right?"

"Wrong."

He looked straight at me. "Seventy dollars for the two. My final offer." He spoke the way he'd spoken to the Times Square Thug. I didn't like it.

"Sorry to have taken your time," I said. I dropped the coin back in my pocket. "I'm not selling."

As I turned to the door he asked, coolly, "You say you got them in Florida?"

"No." I touched the doorknob.

"Wait," he called. I turned toward him. He came around the counter and handed me a business card. "In case you change your mind," he said lightly.

Seeing no reason to be impolite, I took the card and thanked him. "Is there someplace I could reach you?" he asked. "In case I get a buyer who is willing to go higher." The guy was incredibly persistent. In my mind, I raised the coins' value to an even hundred each. He ran back to the counter, got another card and a pen and came back with a friendly smile. I gave him my name and the address at the rooming house in Long Island City. He thanked me and I thanked him and left.

Chapter 6

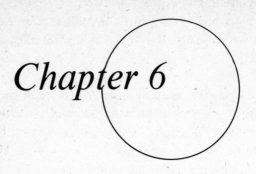

I stood outside the coin guy's store and read his card.

COINS: *OLD AND NEW*
Sean Garfield
Numismatist Extraordinaire
185 W. 47th St. New York
764-2326

Numismatist Extraordinaire. Either Garfield had a sense of humor not apparent on first meeting, or he was mighty sure of himself. I almost went back in to ask him, but rather than give him the idea I was interested in selling, I walked down the street. I stopped in front of another coin store and looked in the dusty window. The shop was about seven feet wide and ten feet deep. An old grey fellow wearing an eyeshade looked up and peered back at me. Desiring a second opinion of my coin, I reached for the door handle. The door was locked. I waved to the old guy. He came forward and asked, through the glass, "What do you want?"

"Could you look at a coin for me?" I asked.

He looked suspicious and frightened. Perhaps the Times Square Thug had visited him as well. I held up one of my coins and asked again. He pressed his nose against the glass and stared. Holding the coin next to the glass, I waited, while his eyes darted from the coin to me. Finally, curiosity seemed to overcome suspicion and he unlocked the door. I thanked him and slipped in. He locked the door behind me and took the coin.

"What do you want to know?" he asked in a thin voice.

"Could you tell me what this is worth?"

"Do you want to sell it?"

"Not really. I found it and another one and I was just wondering what it was."

He glanced at it and handed it back. "Five, perhaps."

I was crushed. "Are you sure?" I asked. "Somebody just told me it was an eighteenth-century doubloon."

"What does he know?" the little man said, turning irritably toward his counter. "It's late seventeenth."

"He offered me forty dollars for it," I persisted.

"He's a crook."

"But you said it's only worth five."

"Five *hundred*," he said acidly.

"Five hundred dollars for this?" I yelled.

"A diamond that size would be worth a million."

"Five hundred dollars?" I repeated weakly.

"Were it dated and the date clear, it might be worth twenty-five thousand."

"And that son of a bitch offered me forty bucks."

"He's a crook."

33

"Look at this," I said. "I have another."

The old man took it in his long fingers. Holding it to the light, and murmuring appreciatively, he said, "Very fine and rather rare."

"What is it?" He seemed a lot more interested in it than the first.

He placed it on the glass counter between us. "Look," he said. Pointing with the tip of a pencil he explained. "See this? The X and the M and the L?"

"Yes?"

"There's a little 'o' missing right before the M. The oMX means this was minted in Mexico. The L was the mark of the mintmaster, in this case Martin Lopez, if I remember right. Now here, this Roman numeral eight means just that. Eight. Eight escudos."

"How old is it?" I asked.

"It's undated, as most of these are, but it must have been minted around 1690, so it would be over . . . two hundred and eighty years old."

"How do you know?"

He turned the doubloon over. "This equal armed cross and this intricate little fleur-de-lis-like object that connects the arms. That's typical of coins minted while Carlos II was king of Spain."

"Oh."

"Also, the planchet, the disk, is short and thick."

"It's not very round," I said.

"Round coins from this era are rare." He looked up, his eyes glowing with his subject. "This piece is really just a weighed and assayed lump of gold stamped to show its value. Round coins were sometimes minted for the king's private coinage. If you find one of them you can retire for a few years."

"What's this one worth?"

The dealer shrugged. "It's rare. Its condition can be described as very fine, which isn't as fine as extra fine . . . Two thousand dollars."

I stood up straight. *"Two thousand dollars?"*

"Of course, if it was extra fine, and it would be if that little 'o' wasn't rubbed out, then it might go for three."

I was stunned. Two thousand dollars was about three months' work and three months' work in a lump is a lot of money for anyone.

He smiled and handed the coin back. "It's a rather nice find for just walking along the beach."

I nodded dumbly. He smiled. "I presume you are not a collector?" he asked.

"No. No, I'm not. And I didn't find it on the beach."

"That's probably where it came from, though. Did you want to sell them?"

"I hadn't really thought about it," I said. "I mean I had no idea they were so valuable." I stared at the coins, not believing my good luck. I watched his face as I said, "They didn't come from the beach."

"Oh?" he said politely.

"They came from the bottom of the East River."

"Oh?" This time he was very interested.

"How do you suppose they got there?" I asked.

"I know how they got there," he said, "but I cannot believe you got them up."

"I'll tell you how I got them up," I said. "If you'll tell me how they got there."

The old man laughed. "That is not a fair bargain, my friend. You can find that out by going to the library. It's common knowledge. But only you can tell me how you got them up."

I hesitated. My encounter with Sean Garfield, Numismatist Extraordinaire, had put me off coin dealers. And now that I knew I had something valuable in my hand I felt somewhat vulnerable. Still, the old guy seemed to be straight.

"I'll even the bargain," he said. "Share with me a pot of tea while I tell you my story. Then, if you like, you can tell me yours." I nodded agreement and he pulled a shade over his window, another over the glass door, and dug out a hot plate and tea kettle and told me his name was Harry Holtzman. Then, as we sat on two high stools over his counter drinking tea, Harry talked.

There had been, he told me, an English pirate named Jonathan Ludlum who had plied the Caribbean capturing Spanish gold ships in the name of the English crown. He had a writ that established his right to privateer. However, larcenous by habit and contentious by nature, he refused to turn in his captured treasure. The English authorities, miffed, had responded by labeling him a pirate, something the Spanish had done the first time they had seen him, and dispatched several ships of the line to deal with him harshly and get back their gold.

As the Spanish had also dispatched ships of the line to do the same thing, Ludlum was forced to leave his Caribbean retreats and head north. Under cover of a tremendous storm, he sailed into New York Harbor to sell what he could of his captured treasure and continue his flight on horseback. Unfortunately the storm that provided cover tore his ship loose from its secret mooring on the upper East River, drove it onto some rocks, and then sank it midstream somewhere between what is now Gracie Mansion and the United Nations.

Treacherous currents and murky water had hidden its exact whereabouts, and salvage attempts had all ended in failure.

"So," Harry concluded, "several million dollars of Spanish gold is scattered over the bottom of the East River, where it will remain forever. Even with modern searching techniques, it will never be found. It's been there for about two hundred and fifty years. You can imagine how the river has covered it over."

"Yes."

Harry refilled our cups. "Your turn," he said. "How did you find the coins?"

"By accident," I said.

"Of course. Don't tell me you were diving in the East River."

"No," I said. "I was under it."

"Under it?"

"Do you know what a sandhog is?" I asked.

"You're digging a tunnel?"

"I'm helping."

"And you found it in the tunnel? Where?"

"Between Welfare Island and Manhattan. In the middle of the river."

"What street will the tunnel touch in Manhattan?"

"Around Sixty-fifth."

"Ah. Tell me," he said, "how far beneath the bottom of the river is the tunnel?"

"About thirty feet."

"Thirty feet," he mused. "It is quite extraordinary."

"It is," I agreed.

"Have any of the other workers found these?"

"Not that I know of," I said.

"Apparently your find was an isolated incident."

"Well, I found these yesterday and there was an accident that closed the tunnel right after that."

"If you find another coin I'll be glad to appraise it for you. I might even buy some if you like."

"Thank you. I might do that."

"I would suggest," he said slowly, "that honesty might not be the best policy in the event you find any more coins."

"What do you mean?"

"The various powers that be would want their cut if your find were known. The state and the city and the tunnel company. So if you happen to find a few more coins, keep it to yourself. You might make a few thousand dollars. The rest of them won't miss it. You know what I mean?" He grinned slyly.

"Got you," I said. "I want to thank you for all the information. You were very kind."

"I've had a pleasant afternoon," Harry said. "Thank you." He unlocked the door and turned to me. "Tell me, who offered you forty dollars for the coin?"

I showed him Sean Garfield Numismatist Extraordinaire's card.

"Him," Harry growled.

I looked askance and Harry explained, "His father built that business. A friend of mine. He died. This Sean is a disappointment."

"I'll avoid him," I said. "Thank you again."

I phoned Jeannie, but she was still out so I told the machine about the coins. Then I caught a cab to take me back to Welfare Island. As I was early I tried Jeannie again.

This time she was in. "Congratulations," she said.

"Thanks. How'd you do today?"

"I had lunch with a producer with hands."

"Oh? Tell him I'd be glad to break them."

"Thanks," Jeannie said. "I took care of him, already."

"How? May I ask?"

"You may. And you can stop worrying about my honor."

"I just don't like some fat slob pawing you for a part."

"He was thin," said Jeannie. "Besides, Howard was with me."

"That's comforting. How'd you get Howard into a restaurant?"

"Lunch was at the producer's house."

I decided to shut up before jealousy made me say something I shouldn't.

"Did you sell the coins?" Jeannie asked.

"I want to hang on to them for a few days."

"Why?"

"I don't know. They're sort of special."

"Well, don't lose them."

"I won't. Let me take you out to dinner tonight. I'm feeling rich."

"Sorry, Hog. Loren's asked me to read for him. Tomorrow night?"

"Sure. I might be very late, though. The tunnel's blocked and I'll probably be on the late shift."

"Tell me when you know."

After I hung up, I decided to go back to Charley's. Rifkins, Kosinski and Burke were still at it, and didn't seem to notice I'd gone farther than the men's room. I caught up with them as the night wore on and had only the vaguest idea the next morning of how I'd gotten home.

I called the hoghouse and they told me to report for the late shift for clean-up work, so I went back to sleep and killed most of the day trying to wake up. Before I left for work I called Jeannie and told her I'd be out around midnight. She said she'd pick me up.

Chapter 7

The tunnel was a mess. Most of the water had been pumped out already, though from what we could see looking down from the catwalks that led from the airlock to the shield, several muddy inches remained at the depths. The harsh string of lights showed that the clean-up crews had finished the heading. Our job was to do the same within the shield itself.

"Do you believe this?" Burke asked when we entered the shield. It looked like a pigsty after a mud slide. No one answered him. We scraped out the worst of the mud, which filled two battleships, and sent them on their way before we'd reached the front of the shield, fifteen feet from the door.

Once at the diaphragm, the front cutting edge, Rifkins ordered Kosinski and Burke to clean up the hydraulic jacks while I was to keep shoveling mud. Always me.

Nobody ever gave me cushy jobs like cleaning jacks. I was the dependable mud shoveler. Cursing quietly, I began to fill another battleship.

But, after two shovelfuls, I stopped cursing. In fact, for several seconds I stopped breathing. And I stopped shoveling, which was a mistake because Rifkins yelled. Frantically I shoveled. The last thing in the world I needed was to have Rifkins see the mud. He stopped when he saw me resume my labors.

As soon as his back was turned, I poked the mud experimentally with my shovel. It was filled with rocks. Or what looked like rocks, but which were, I knew—I hoped—not rocks. Pulling some of the mud away, I saw that the deeper I dug into it the heavier the concentration of rocks. Glancing around to make sure no one was watching, I jabbed the blade of the shovel against a rock.

It fell apart. I bent down and picked up the core that remained. It seemed just like the first two rocks that had turned out to be coins. I looked over my shoulder. Burke and Kosinski and Rifkins were ten feet away, their backs turned toward me, toiling over a jack. Their heavy breathing and muttered curses indicated they'd run into some kind of a problem. I sliced the shovel through another rock. The same thing happened. The outer crust fell away, revealing a disk-shaped core that had to be something other than rock. I picked it up, and spit on it to soften the mud. Some of the mud came off, but I couldn't tell for sure what was inside.

There seemed to be about a hundred similar lumps in the mud before me. Curious, I opened another door in the shield and checked out its contents. For several seconds I stared. I couldn't believe it. The cavity behind the door was jammed solid with lumps of varying sizes.

They were stuck together so tightly there was hardly any mud between them. I shut the door and opened another. The same thing.

The shield had apparently moved smack into a wall of mud-encrusted coins. Or what I hoped was coins, though I had no way of making sure until I got them out. Then, with sickening certitude, I realized there was no way I *could* get them out. There were hundreds of them, maybe thousands. And Rifkins was sure to question my intent if I carried mud and rocks out of the tunnel in my arms instead of using the more conventional means at hand.

"Creegan!"

I jumped, slammed the door shut and turned all at once. As I completed my gyrations, I hollered loudly and respectfully, "Yes?"

"Get your ass over here!" It was Rifkins bellowing, who else? I thought he had seen me poking around in the mud again. I darted toward him apprehensively.

"Grab that and pull." He and Burke were tugging at something while Kosinski manipulated a big screwdriver.

"Not that, you damned fool. *That.*"

I dropped the first thing and pulled something else. Kosinski fiddled with the screwdriver. Then he nodded some secret signal to Rifkins, who nodded back and yelled, "Pull, you guys. Pull!"

We pulled and nothing happened. Finally Burke said, "Nothing's happening." He let go of the shaft and stood up. I followed his lead, kneading my hands into the small of my back to ease some of the painful activity going on there. Kosinski shook his head. Rifkins swore and told me to get back to the shoveling. Then he bent back over the recalcitrant jack and resumed his cryptic head movements with Kosinski. Burke leaned against a stanchion and ignored everything.

I got back to my discovery at the face of the shield, wondering if I had found some more of Ludlum's treasure.

It would be worth something if it was mine. At the moment it was in the tunnel and, as Harry had said, the Tunnel People—which included the Metropolitan Tunnel Company People, and the City of New York People, not to mention the Long Island Railroad People for whom we were digging the tunnel—were likely to claim it would be worth something for them. I wondered what my cut would be if I just reported to Rifkins that I'd found pirate treasure. Something told me I'd be ceremoniously presented with a single gold coin mounted on a plaque that attested to my long and faithful service to the Metropolitan Tunnel Company and the City of New York, not to mention the Long Island Railroad.

That would never do. If I could get out even a portion of the lumps of mud before me, I'd do all right for myself and wouldn't have to worry about money or a job for a long time. I liked that idea. Unfortunately, getting out a portion would be no easier than getting out all of it. I could cram some into my pockets, but how could I tell which lumps were valuable and which were not?

The problem was that things left the tunnel in two ways. Well, three, if you count things flying out during a blowout, but we won't count that. Basically, living things passed through the airlock at the beginning of the tunnel. It was situated on the top half of the tunnel. Beneath it was another airlock for nonliving things. The living things were sandhogs and the occasional civil engineer.

The nonliving things were the battleships carrying mud and rocks out and materials in. As I've explained, people have to decompress when they leave the tunnel. On this particular job, that was taking the better part of an hour. But the sand and mud, of course, didn't have to go through that process, so the battleships just passed through the airlock and on their way. There was also an emergency lock, but when that was used, half the world was waiting on the other side to see what had gone wrong.

"Hey, what's that stuff?" Burke suddenly spoke four inches from my ear and I knew I was caught.

Chapter 8

"What stuff?"

Burke pointed at the pile like an eager red setter. "That stuff."

"You mean these rocks?"

"Funny-looking rocks," Burke said. He edged closer. "How come you're not putting them in the battleship?"

"I was. I am. See?" I shoveled several mad strokes. The rocks clattered into the steel container. Burke looked on suspiciously, then, in his incomparably loud voice, said, "Funny thing, hitting rocks. Them's the first we've seen since we left the bank." The geologists had predicted mud for the entire passage under the East River.

"Funny," I laughed, contriving to look like I was shoveling a lot more than I was, and painfully aware that each load I dropped into the battleship could have been worth thousands of dollars. When the hopper was filled, a fortune would pass down the tunnel and into oblivion.

Unfortunately, Burke didn't move. And as I continued to pile smaller and smaller amounts of debris into the hopper, his truculent suspicion grew. Finally he couldn't hold himself in.

"Creegan. What the devil are you doing?"

I straightened up and faced him. "What do you mean?"

"A nine-year-old kid at the beach shovels more than you do," he observed. "Put your back into it."

"I hadn't heard you were made foreman."

Burke's face darkened like a mineshaft. "Pray I never am, Creegan. Least not on your crew."

"I'm praying," I said lightly, forcing a grin onto my face to ease his anger. Burke had obviously wanted to be foreman for some time. I couldn't have said anything much worse if I'd spent time thinking about it.

"Relax," I said quietly. "You're right. I'm not shoveling enough. I hurt my back."

"Oh. I'm so sorry." His voice was not sincere.

I shopped around for some kind of answer that would send him away and give me time to think. "I appreciate your concern," I said. "And now, unless you want something, I shall return to my labors."

Burke's face purpled deeper. His eyes were beady and red. I had forgotten I was dealing with a man with a tremendous headache and hangover. He looked like he was about to forget the ironclad law that said anybody who got into a fight in the tunnel was fired immediately. I wasn't interested in fighting, for any one of a number of reasons, so I looked around for something to divert him.

It came, unexpectedly, in the form of our leader. Rifkins rose from the stuck jack and saw Burke and me

47

nose to nose at the front of the shield. "Burke," he yelled. "Grab this." He indicated the same steel shaft we'd been tugging at before. Burke spun on his heel, strode toward the jack and gripped the shaft with his tremendous hands. I started to follow but Rifkins waved me off and said he'd call me when he needed me. I said O.K. and returned to my treasure.

I opened several of the doors in the shield and stared inside. Then I closed them and tried to make my brain come up with a solution. The tunnel was like a jail. There was no alternate way of leaving that I could think of. I glanced down through the catwalks to the bottom of the shaft, and then up to the curved ceiling, where the tremendous curved iron plates already in place formed the roof. Above that was thirty feet of mud and then the bottom of the river.

There had to be another way.

There was. And when it came to me I was startled by how greedy I had been. It involved some risk and a lot of fast talking, but it might work. So, cautiously, I approached Rifkins, who was bending over Kosinski, who was slowly shaking his head back and forth.

Burke noticed me and glowered but didn't say anything. Rifkins was engrossed with the jack. I waited next to him for some sign of recognition. When I was about to say something, he suddenly yelled, "Creegan!"

I said, "I'd like to talk to you."

"Pull that," he commanded. I kept standing and calculated how long we had been down. It was less than an hour, which meant we had a little over two hours to do what had to be done. That didn't leave me much time for pulling on jacks.

"Rifkins," I said sharply. "Listen to me."

"Pull."

Burke bent over and tugged. I said again, "Listen, Rifkins. We have a problem."

"Pull."

"Rifkins," I yelled and pounded his muscular back with my open hand. He looked up, confused. "I have to talk to you," I said. He shook his head disbelievingly.

"Later," he snapped, and turned away. Burke pulled and Rifkins suddenly yelled to stop. Burke stopped and straightened up. I started to pound Rifkins's back again and thought better of it. He was muttering a steady barrage of curses concerning everything in his immediate vicinity. Kosinski shook his head. Rifkins leaned closer and asked something.

I stepped back, caught Burke's eye and motioned him away. He glared suspiciously for a moment, cast a glance at Rifkins's back and followed me to the front of the shield.

"What's your problem?"

"I want to show you something."

"What were you trying to say to Rifkins?"

"What I'm going to show you. Look." I picked up a likely looking lump and rubbed it against the side of the battleship until the outer mud was gone. "This," I said without ceremony, "is probably a gold coin. It is probably worth about a thousand bucks."

Burke looked at the lump. He looked at me. He passed his hand over his obviously throbbing temples. I waited for him to say something like "You're kidding," or "You're full of it," or "You're putting me on" or "Very funny."

Instead he asked, "A thousand bucks?"

"Maybe more. Maybe less. Something like that."

"How do you know that?" he asked coolly.

"I'll explain later. I know it."

"How did it get here?"

"It was in the river mud. It's pirate treasure." I was aware of the ludicrous sound of that phrase. Pirate treasure conjures up some silly images.

"Is that right?" Burke asked.

"It is," I said. "But we've got a problem."

"Getting it out," Burke said.

I stared at him, somewhat astonished that he had accepted everything I had said without a doubt. And he knew instantly the problem. I was glad already I had thought of including everyone.

"We've got another problem," I said.

"How much you figure is here?" Burke asked. His voice was excited.

"If there are a thousand rocks here that's a million bucks."

"There's at least a thousand," Burke said with a gulp.

"They are not all necessarily gold. Some might be silver. Some might just be chunks of metal."

"All not gold?"

"We can't be sure," I said, hastily adding that if half were gold we'd still be rich. "But there's another problem," I said.

"What?" Burke was no longer looking at me. His beady eyes had grown wide and he couldn't take them off the pile of rocks.

"Whose side is Rifkins on?" I asked.

"What? Whose sides are there?"

"The finders and the keepers," I answered.

"What the hell is that supposed to mean?"

"Keep your voice down. It means that we're the

finders and, if we don't play this cool, the company's going to be the keepers. You get it?"

"Oh," Burke said and a cunning look spread over his face. His hangover seemed to vanish and with it his nasty mood. "I don't think that's the way we want it to be."

"Agreed. Now whose side is Rifkins on?"

"Jees," said Burke. "Ours, I guess. Why wouldn't he be?"

"He's the foreman. He's company."

"Well, he's not a damned fool."

"I don't know. What if he is?"

"If he is," Burke said seriously, "he may have an unfortunate accident with that hydraulic jack he's working on."

"Wait. Wait. Wait. Now don't go getting all upset and killing someone. Christ, Burke."

"A million dollars," Burke said evenly, "is not leaving this tunnel for the company."

I struggled for words to meet a situation I hadn't imagined, but Burke elbowed me and snapped, "He's coming."

Rifkins moved toward us. It seemed as if he'd been watching us for some time. He couldn't have heard anything, but he looked suspicious.

"All right, boys. What's up?"

"Get the jack freed?" Burke asked.

"I said what's up."

"I think we'd better have a little talk," I said. Rifkins looked down at me. Sweat streamed from his face and soaked his light shirt. He was breathing normally, though the past two days' drinking was showing itself in the ninety degree compressed air heat.

Rifkins came right to the point. "Wildcats are illegal.

You got a grievance, you take it up through the proper channels. But no screwing around in the tunnel."

"Wildcat?" I asked.

"No strikes in the tunnel," Rifkins said adamantly. "Now get back to work." He glared a moment for emphasis, then wheeled toward the jack that Kosinski labored over. Burke grabbed his arm and spun him around. Rifkins looked at Burke's hand on his arm in shocked disbelief. Then, taking Burke's wrist between his thumb and forefinger, he said, "Let go," in a voice that carried all the force of the largest sandhog foreman on the East Coast of the United States of America.

Burke refused to acknowledge the threat. "Listen to what Creegan says."

Rifkins just got calmer, though his face reddened. "I think you and Creegan better get back to work."

Burke stepped closer and grabbed Rifkins with both hands, shaking him as vigorously as someone the size of Rifkins could be shaken.

"Listen, you damned fool. Creegan's going to make you rich." He bared his teeth and shouted an inch from Rifkins's chin. "Now listen." With that he released Rifkins, who was beginning to wind up like the main spring on Big Ben. I stepped closer and spoke rapidly.

"There's gold in the shield. You and me and Burke and Kosinski can share it if we can get it the hell out of here before somebody else finds it. It's maybe worth a million bucks, maybe more, maybe less, and . . ."

"What are you, crazy?" Rifkins snapped and turned away. I grabbed his arm and tried to pull him back around. Burke grabbed his other arm and together we slowly turned him. I felt his muscles tense and he started to throw us off.

"I'm not crazy," I yelled. "You are. Listen!"

Then, like the rumble that announces tons of water entering a blown tunnel, three words boomed across the shield.

"LET HIM GO!"

Before I could do anything I felt my hands ripped from Rifkins, and a second later went spinwheeling across the shield. Burke joined me.

Standing like two bull elephants aligned against the jackals were Rifkins and Kosinski. The look of almost maternal solicitude on Kosinski's face would have gone down a lot better if Rifkins were the kind of guy who needed protection. It was as if Russia and China had signed a mutual assistance pact in the event of an attack by Rhode Island.

Burke called across no man's land, "I guess you overheard, Kosinski. That's good. You can help us explain to Rifkins about the gold."

Rifkins looked suspiciously at his protector. "What do you know about this?"

"Gold?" said Kosinski.

"Tell him," Burke yelled.

"That's right," I yelled. "Tell him how we can get it out if we work together."

"You know about this?" Rifkins asked.

"Gold!" Burke screamed. "Gold! Gold!"

Kosinski shook his massive head and smiled. "Gold?"

"How come you didn't tell me?" Rifkins asked.

"You wouldn't listen!" Burke roared.

"How did it get here?" Rifkins asked.

"A pirate ship sank in the river and the treasure was lost in the mud. We ran into it."

"Where is it?" Rifkins asked, looking around.

"Where is it?" Kosinski asked.

"Right there," said I, pointing at the pile of mud.

Rifkins shambled over. "I don't see no gold."

"It's crusted with mud," I said wearily. "Take my word for it."

"Believe it," said Rifkins. "I want to see it."

"We don't have much time," I said.

"What's the rush?" Rifkins asked belligerently. I shared an agonized grimace with Burke and tried to explain the situation. "This treasure," I began, "is gold coins that are about three hundred years old. Each coin is worth a lot of money. Anything between five hundred and many thousands, depending upon how rare it is. A coin expert can tell you the difference, I can't. O.K?"

"How'd it get here?" Rifkins looked skeptical.

"A pirate ship sank in the river."

Rifkins laughed harshly. "Just like that? And landed right in front of the heading?"

"Remember the wood we found right before the blow?"

His face sobered. "Yeah."

"I think we ran into the ship."

"Yeah," said Kosinski. "A couple of guys up top said they found some timbers in the heading."

"See?" I said.

"I didn't hear that," said Rifkins.

"You saw the wood in the mud?"

"O.K. Suppose it happened." His eyes narrowed as if he were trying to fill in the spaces that bothered him. "How come you know all this?"

"Because," I said, "I found a couple of these in the tunnel the day before yesterday and I took them to a coin dealer and he told me about the coins and the lost treasure. O.K.?"

"Lemme see the coin," Rifkins growled.

"It's in my locker," I said. "I don't have it with me."

"So show me one of the new ones," Rifkins said.

"Here." I dropped a muddy lump in his hand.

"What the hell?"

"It's in the mud," I said. "It takes a while to scrape it off. And we don't have much more time."

"What's the rush?" Rifkins iterated.

"We have to leave the tunnel in about an hour and a half. That's not much time."

"For what?" Rifkins asked. A truculent look was spreading over his face. I wondered how dumb he could be. Then he handed the lump I'd handed him to Kosinski. "See if you can find anything in this," he said quietly. Kosinski took it without a word.

Burke hopped around impatiently. The mad gleam the first mention of gold had brought to his eye was back bright and clear. Before I could stop him he tapped Rifkins on the chest and asked, "Whose side you on, Rifkins?"

"What?"

"Finders or keepers?"

"What?"

"You want to keep this gold or not?" Burke yelled and danced madly in a circle.

"What do you mean, keep it?"

"He means," I said, shoving Burke behind me, "we can keep this gold for ourselves and split a million bucks, or we can tell everybody we found it and split it with the tunnel company and the city and the railroad."

"Oh?" Rifkins said, puzzlement replacing truculence. "Oh. Well, the company . . ."

"Screws," Burke finished for him, "every one of us and you know it. This gold is ours. Ours." He pounded his chest for emphasis.

I shoved Burke back behind me and looked Rifkins in the eye. "It's a lot of money for *four* of us," I said.

"And diddlysquat if we share it with every bastard in the state," Burke yelled over my shoulder.

I turned and said, "Shut up." Then I turned back and met Rifkins's eye and saw what I was afraid I'd see. Fear. His eyes were yelling, what if we get caught? What happens to me and my job and my pension?

Burke darted to the pile and scooped up an armload of mud. "This is sandhog gold," he yelled. "Sandhog gold. Not company gold. It's ours. Ours."

"I don't know," Rifkins said hesitantly.

"Sandhog gold," Burke stormed, mud running down his shirt and pants. "We slave down here. We risk our lives building tunnels for them fat asses in the limousines. We grub around down here while the brass screw their secretaries. We get the bends while those bastards get blow jobs under their desks. This is our frigging gold." He clutched the muddy lumps tightly and glared maniacally at Rifkins and me.

I looked at Rifkins. "He's right, you know," I said. "We deserve it."

Rifkins started to say something but Kosinski came up behind him and tapped his shoulder. Then he extended in his palm what he'd discovered in the lump. It was a twisted piece of grey metal.

"Gold?" asked Kosinski.

Chapter 9

"Lead!" screamed Burke.

"Lead," said Rifkins, sounding relieved and disappointed at the same time.

"Lead?" asked Kosinski, fondling the little lead chip.

"Let me see that," I said.

Burke leaped at me, grabbed my shirt with both hands, and slammed me back against a bulkhead. I started to disengage myself, but Kosinski and Rifkins surrounded me and listened intently for my answer after Burke yelled, "What's this crap, Creegan?"

"A fitting," I said hastily. "Part of the boat."

"Where's the gold?" Burke asked, tightening his grip. He'd dropped his armload of muddy lumps, and his dripping shirt plastered mine brown. I brought both hands up quickly onto his wrists, breaking his grip. He still held parts of my collar in each hand. He leaped as if to grab again, but Rifkins stopped him. Rifkins looked at me sternly and said, "This was a big joke."

"No joke," said I.

"Where is the gold?" Kosinski asked menacingly.

"It wasn't very funny," Rifkins said thoughtfully.

"What do you care?" I asked. "You were all ready to give it to the company."

"It *was* a joke," Burke howled. "I'll kill him."

"Not in the tunnel," Rifkins said.

"Thanks," I said.

"No gold?" Kosinski said mournfully.

"I wouldn't really have given it to the company," Rifkins said. "I would have changed my mind."

"Then change it," I snapped. "We're wasting time."

"Don't start again," Rifkins warned.

"Let's kill him now," Burke raged. Little droplets of saliva were forming at the corners of his mouth.

"No," Rifkins said. "Get back to work."

"Can't we just beat him up?" Burke asked plaintively.

"Not in the tunnel. I told you already."

"Later," Kosinski muttered. "When we go up top."

"SHUT UP ALL OF YOU!" I yelled as loud as I could. It stunned them silent. "This piece Kosinski cleaned off was a little bit of metal that probably came from the ship that sank. Maybe it was a fitting on a chest, or a tool, or maybe it was part of the ship itself. But that doesn't mean there is no gold. There are tons of gold. Thousands of pieces were on the ship. Thousands. Now we're not going to find all of it, I don't think. But we sure as hell can take out a lot, if, and I repeat, *if* you guys will stop screwing around and get busy on getting the stuff out of here."

I looked at three very suspicious faces. Suspicion turned to anger within seconds. Then to rage.

"You just don't know when to stop," Rifkins said quietly. "I think you have gone too far."

"Let's beat him up," Kosinski said. I cringed. He sounded very serious.

"Come on," said Burke. "We can kill him. We'll say he fell off a scaffold and landed on his head. Kosinski? Hand me a shovel. You hold him. I'll bash his head in."

"No," I said.

"No," Rifkins said.

"Thank you," I breathed. Rifkins looked at me as if I'd just crawled out of the slime. It was time for yelling again and some action.

"LOOK!" I yelled, stopping quickly to pick up four lumps. "Everybody clean one of these off and then decide if I'm lying." I passed a lump to each man and kept one for myself. Then, ignoring the others, I stepped off to a quiet corner and began scraping the mud with my knife. As it fell away I looked up. Rifkins, Burke and Kosinski had each retired to a private spot to do the same. They concentrated mightily, scraping with knives and screwdrivers. Burke slammed his lump several times into the side of the battleship. It echoed hollowly in the shield.

I looked up at the naked light bulbs and prayed I'd find gold. But the more I scraped, the less disk-like my lump became. More and more it began to resemble a nail. Make it a gold nail, I prayed. But it wasn't. It was a nail that on closer inspection looked like a badly eroded brass screw. A horrible thought occurred to me, that there was no gold. Only bits and pieces of poor Pirate Ludlum's ship.

"Gold my ass," Burke suddenly snorted. "Look at this crap."

I didn't step closer for a look. Rather, I began planning ways I could avoid the three of them for the duration of our stay in the shield. Burke was already making his way toward me. He looked around, apparently seeking a weapon. Then, with a chilling smile, he remembered the knife he was holding in his hand.

"Gold," said Kosinski. "It's gold."

"Bull," said Burke and kept coming toward me.

Rifkins shot a hand out and grabbed Burke by the neck, effectively ending his homicidal intentions. "Mine's gold too," he said quietly. "Creegan wasn't lying." Letting Burke go, Rifkins compared pieces with Kosinski. Then, grinning, the two of them approached me and held up their finds.

"These like your coin, Creegan?"

"Look just like it," I said. "I really don't know much about them, but they look the same. And it's definitely gold."

"Good," said Kosinski.

"GOLD!" shrieked Burke. "It's gold. We're rich."

"Now can we get started?" I asked.

Burke stuck his knife back in his boot and scooped me up in a bear hug. Bouncing me up and down, he spewed sour beer and whiskey breath in my face and yelled, "You did it, Creegan, you did it." For a horrifying second I thought he'd kiss me. Over his shoulder I saw Rifkins's face play with doubts and fears. Burke dropped me suddenly and broke into a coughing fit. I darted to Rifkins and told him we had to get started salvaging the gold. Before he could argue, I reminded him he had said he was willing to go through with it. Kosinski nodded vigorously, and slowly Rifkins relaxed. Finally he said, "All right. We'll do it. But we got to be careful."

"There's no risk," I said.

"How do we get it out?" Rifkins asked. "You said you knew a way."

"There's only one way," I said. "It's risky—wait, let me finish. There is some risk we'll lose the stuff. But no chance of anybody finding out what we're doing."

"How?" Rifkins asked cautiously. Burke had stopped coughing and was madly stuffing his pockets with mud lumps. He looked like a kid on Halloween night who'd forgotten his goody sack.

"Not like that," I said to Rifkins. "We can't carry enough. Everybody will see we're up to something, and as we just found out, not all of the lumps are worth anything."

"Yeah, what about that?" Rifkins replied.

"Yeah?" Kosinski muttered, puzzlement screwing up his face.

"We have to take every damned single lump out of here. Every one. And pray nobody finds any more in the next shift."

"They won't know what they are," Rifkins said.

"Hopefully not," I replied. "But we still have to take all we can find because we can't tell which are the good ones."

"We can't carry them with us," Rifkins said. "There's too many."

"We'll send them out in the battleship," I said.

"What?"

"What?" Kosinski echoed Rifkins. Rifkins jerked his

head toward Burke. "Kosinski, make Burke empty his pockets." Kosinski went over to Burke and I explained that the battleship was the only way out. Then I said, "As near as I can remember, the battleship goes up the elevator on the other side of the airlock and then is dumped in a barge. Am I right?"

Rifkins furrowed his massive brow and pondered. "Jees, Creegan, I *think* so. I can't remember for sure. Who notices what's going on up top?"

"I'm almost positive," I said. "The barge is tied up down from the entrance. The battleship reaches it on a little railway line down here."

"So we just go over to the barge and get the gold out of it?"

"Right."

"But it'll be an hour before we can reach it. It will be covered up something awful."

"No," I smiled. "That's the one good luck we have. We'll send the gold out just before we leave the shield. And nobody will send any more mud out until we've decompressed, and they've compressed. We'll have nearly an hour to get there."

"But the barge has people on it. What about the guy who dumps the battleships? There's probably floodlights and everything."

"We can take care of the lights," I said casually. "Cut a cable or something. We'll need some dark to work in."

"Sabotage," Rifkins breathed. He looked outraged and scared at once.

"It's not exactly that serious," I said. "Just one little cut."

"You can't go around destroying company property," Rifkins said fiercely.

"After we get the *gold,*" I said softly, "we can send the company an anonymous donation to cover the expenses. How about that?"

"I'm not sure," Rifkins said, but he was wavering.

"It's the only way. We'll need time to locate the gold, sift it out of the mud that's already there, and get it out and load it into something."

"What?"

"One of our cars?"

"I don't have mine here," Rifkins said.

"You had it yesterday," I remembered.

"It's in the body shop," Rifkins muttered and looked away. A moment later he said, "I ran into a truck when we left Charley's." He was embarrassed. It occurred to me I never knew how strait-laced he was.

"We'll use somebody else's," I said.

"Yours."

"I don't have one."

"Neither does Burke or Kosinski."

"Forget it," I said. "We'll steal a truck."

"*Steal* a truck?"

"Just borrow it. For a little while. We'll bring it right back."

"I don't know about that."

"A million bucks split four ways is a quarter of a million bucks for each of us," I said. "That's two hundred and fifty thousand dollars."

"Maybe we could borrow one for a little while," Rifkins said.

"Good. Let's get the battleship loaded."

"Hang on," said Kosinski. "This stuff'll be scattered all over the barge. How we going to find it?"

"Yeah," said Burke.

I looked around the shield. "We'll bag it," I said, taking my knife from my pocket. There were nine or ten sandbags left over from the blow. I slit one open and poured the sand into the muck below. Kosinski, Burke and Rifkins grabbed their knives and followed suit.

"What if the guy dumping the battleship sees the bags?" asked Rifkins.

"If you spent your life emptying battleships, would you watch what comes out?"

Rifkins shook his head. Kosinski persuaded Burke to empty his pockets by threatening to pound him into jelly if he didn't. Then we emptied the battleship of the gold and mud I'd already put into it and began to fill the bags.

We worked by hand. Burke picked lumps from the pile on the deck and then from the hatches in the shield. He handed them to Kosinski, who knocked off loose mud and handed them to Rifkins, who loaded them into the bags, which he handed to me. I lowered them into the battleship.

We had two of the hoppers in with us. We figured we could fill one with the gold, and the other with the mud we were charged with removing from the shield. Rifkins pointed out that as well as getting our gold out, we had to perform the clean-up if we weren't going to get flak when we got out. As far as I was concerned this would be my last time in the shield, but I agreed with Rifkins that we had to make things look normal.

We ran out of bags before we were done so we dumped the remaining lumps in loose, because it was better to get them all out of the tunnel than risk someone finding them. Rifkins and I counted as we loaded and had reached eighteen hundred and forty-seven when Burke announced that we had them all.

The pile came to about a foot from the top of the battleship. I figured roughly that at an average weight per lump of two to three ounces, we had about three hundred pounds of lumps, and perhaps a hundred pounds of gold, minus those lumps which weren't gold. And a hundred pounds of gold—just as gold, regardless of coins—was worth about a hundred and fifty thousand dollars. How much the coins were worth was staggering.

"O.K.," Rifkins said, fully the foreman again. "Cover them up with mud. About six inches." I grabbed a shovel to do what I was told.

"Wait," said Burke.

"What's the matter. You find more?"

"No. Look, you guys. Just in case something goes wrong. Just in case we can't find the gold."

"We'll find it," I said. "It's got to be right on top of the muck pile."

"But just in case, let's take some insurance."

"No gold in the pockets," Rifkins said. "Somebody'll notice and we'll be up the creek."

"Just a few," Burke pleaded. "Maybe a few thousand bucks in case something goes wrong."

"No."

"One in each pocket?"

Rifkins relented. We were all watching him, hopefully, and what Burke said made sense. A thousand bucks or so was better than nothing. But, Rifkins said, just the front pockets. We could take two, one for each pocket. No one argued. Cautiously we surrounded the battleship and looked in.

"Hurry it up," Rifkins warned. "We still gotta clean up this mess. We got less than a half hour to go."

I looked into the battleship and tried to pick two likely

lumps. The other three guys did the same. The trouble was, how could we know the good from the bad? Kosinski, after staring a second, just dropped in one large paw and took the first two he touched. That seemed as sensible as any other way so I did the same, placing a muddy lump carefully in each front pants pocket.

Rifkins, who'd hurried us along, hesitated. He seemed to be trying to see through the mud as he bent over the battleship. Licking his lips, he glanced all around, then impulsively took one lump from the left near corner and the other from the far right. He hefted them in his hand a moment, then, with a resigned shrug, placed them in his pockets.

Burke still hadn't made his choice. His face was flushed with anxious greed. He pursed his lips and extended two pudgy fingers, much like a chubby matron searching for the cherry-filled chocolate in a box of assorted sweets. Tentatively he touched a lump, started to pick it up, then recoiled as if it were hot, his eyes having suddenly fallen on a more likely specimen. He poked that, cupped it in his palm, and weighed it speculatively. Craftily, he laid it on the edge of the battleship and searched for another.

Rifkins put up with that for another minute, after which he told Burke to make his choice and get out of the way. When Burke continued to vacillate, Rifkins began shoveling mud over the whole load. Slowly, as Kosinski and I watched, and Burke scrabbled frantically through the remaining uncovered parts, the battleship filled. Soon it looked like any ordinary hopper full of muck. Rifkins tapped one of Burke's fingers with his shovel.

Pouting, Burke finally made his choice. The rest of the coins were covered with mud. I picked up a sledge hammer and dealt the battleship a solid smack. Before the enormous boom stopped reverberating off the cast iron and steel tunnel lining, I delivered an equally hard second shot on the same spot.

Rifkins asked what I was doing. I pointed out that it might be handy to be able to recognize this particular battleship among the many others on the site that were all the same, except that they weren't filled with gold. Rifkins agreed, though he remarked he thought there might have been a less destructive way of doing it. I fingered the impressive dent my sledge had made and told him I was sorry.

We spent the next twenty minutes doing the work we should have done in two and a half hours. Rifkins kept yelling that we had to make it look like things were normal. One of the nice things, probably the only nice thing, about working in compressed air is that no one pops in on you unexpectedly to see if you're working hard enough. With the exception of a telephone, we had no outside contact.

When it was time to go into the airlock, we lined up our gold-laden battleship at the door to the materials airlock, right behind the muck-filled one. Quickly we shoved the muck car into the airlock. Our special car was next, but no one seemed to want to touch it.

"Shove it in," Rifkins ordered.

No one moved.

"Hell," he snorted, "I'll do it myself."

"Wait," said Burke. "Why don't we all do it together?"

Everyone stared at him.

"Well, you know. Make it a ceremony. For good luck and everything. Come on."

Avoiding each other's eyes, we placed our hands on

the battleship and, as Burke counted, "one, two, three, shove," we shoved. It glided heavily and smoothly along its shiny rails into the darkness of the materials airlock. For a moment we all stared after it.

"I wish I could ride along with it," Burke said.

"Go ahead," said Rifkins, as he heaved the door shut. "Then we'll only have to split three ways."

Chapter 10

I'll never work in a shield again, I thought as I went into the decompression airlock. I sat down on the bench and watched Burke swing the steel door shut. That was it. My last view of the hot, dangerous, circular pit I'd worked in for seven years. With the boom of the closing door and the sharp snapping of the latches and the hiss of air a period of my life had ended. I had no regrets. To live comfortably on my share of a million bucks of coins seemed far preferable to what I'd been doing.

We hadn't done the usual back-breaking work that shift, having spent a lot of time talking and arguing and arranging coins in the battleship, and consequently I didn't feel the usual exhaustion. But for several minutes I sat alone and didn't speak. I thought about the years in the shield and how I'd gotten into it in the first place. I did it for my old man—or at least that's what I thought at the time. I was eighteen and big enough to work, though I hadn't reached full strength. I'd been with him as long as I could remember and, because I knew he was proud of me, and didn't know it was the pride of love, I signed up with a tunnel crew one time while he was away. By the time he returned I was a sandhog. He told me before he died that if he'd known he would have tried to talk me out of it. He didn't really believe it was the type of work a father should pass on to his son.

He told me the trouble was that it was so hard to get out. You reach a point where you have this one skill and people pay you a hell of a lot of money for performing it and then it's too late. You can't do better anywhere else. Also, as with anything really dangerous and difficult, you're part of a select group of people, and ordinary work doesn't have the same feeling. Sandhogs, hard-rock miners, salvage divers and iron workers, all of us, we can't just work on an assembly line or drive a truck. But I knew now what had bothered him most. After all was said and done, all I really did was shovel mud.

I wondered what I'd do with all my money.

"You did say a million bucks," Burke suddenly called from the door. He wiped a gauge with his sleeve and grinned.

"Give or take a few hundred thousand," I answered.

"A million bucks," Burke said dreamily.

"A quarter of a million bucks," Rifkins reminded him.

"Do you know what you can do with a million bucks?" Burke asked the group at large.

"A quarter of a million bucks," Kosinski said sternly.

Burke winked at me. "Hey, Kosinski," he called, "what you going to spend your money on?"

Kosinski answered without hesitation. "A farm."

Burke laughed. "You want to scratch around on a dirt farm? Kosinski, you're kidding. A farm?"

"What's wrong with that?" Rifkins asked.

"Nothing," Burke said. "I just can't believe Kosinski wants to muck around on a farm. That's just like working."

"What's wrong with working?" Kosinski asked.

Burke laughed.

"What about you?" Rifkins asked him.

"Me?" Burke said. "With a million bucks, I'll buy everything in the world. Cars, women, a big boat. Mostly women. You guys ever been in the whorehouses in Taiwan? Best in the world. And Vegas. I'm going to rent so many broads I'll need a personnel office."

"A quarter of a million," I said.

"Yeah. Right. A quarter of a million bucks. Jees I'm going to have fun." He twisted an air valve and chuckled to himself. Kosinski sat solidly silent, staring across the chamber. Rifkins looked vaguely uncomfortable. Burke laughed some more and asked Rifkins what he would do.

"We don't have it yet," Rifkins said nervously.

"It's in the bag," Burke said. "In the bag. Come on, Rifkins, what you going to do?"

"If I get my money," Rifkins said, "and I don't have it yet, if I get it I'm going to learn to fly."

"You're too heavy," Burke said.

Rifkins shut his mouth.

"What's with you guys?" Burke yelled. "You should be happy."

"We're happy," I said.

"Show it," Burke said.

"I'm going to buy a plane," Rifkins said. "And I'm going to take flying lessons."

"That sounds nice," I said. "What kind of a plane?"

"Single engine Apache," he said. "I'll use it for charter. Take hunters up to Canada, that sort of thing."

We all turned toward him. "You sound like you've been planning this," I said.

Rifkins smiled. It broke over his harsh face like the sun after a storm. "I have. I've been saving my money. But I didn't expect to have enough for quite a while." It was the first I'd heard of it. Burke looked equally surprised, though Kosinski gravely nodded his head and I realized Rifkins had shared his plans with him.

Burke barked, "You, too. Just like Kosinski. What's with this working thing? Christ, Rifkins, you're forty if you're a day and you want to go into business."

"Thirty-eight," Rifkins said.

"Doesn't anybody just want to relax?" Burke asked. "What about you, Creegan? You going into business too?"

"Not likely," I said.

"Then what are you going to do?"

"I haven't thought about it too much, maybe I'll go out to California."

"What's in California? You were there on the BART tunnel."

"Yeah. But someone's going out there and where that someone goes I'd like to be."

"The broad with the funny car?"

"That's the one."

"Looked pretty good," Burke observed.

"I'll tell her you said so."

"But it don't cost any two hundred and fifty thousand bucks to go to California."

"I'll need a place to stay," I said.

Burke snorted. "Trouble with you guys is you don't got no imagination."

"Trouble with you," Rifkins said, "is you got too much." He looked around at the three of us. "We don't have that money yet. We might lose our jobs over this move and then you'll see what happens."

"But we won't lose the money," Burke said grimly.

"He's right," I said quickly. "We can't lose the coins. They'll be right on top of the muck on the barge."

"Look," Rifkins said seriously, very much the foreman. "I don't want any of you guys charging straight out of this chamber and down to the barge. You hear?"

"We're not charging anyplace," I agreed, glad to hear Rifkins was keeping his cool. "We don't want to do anything to draw attention to ourselves."

"I was just going to say that," Rifkins said. "We got to act natural. Otherwise we'll get caught in the wrong place and get fired."

"Otherwise," I said, "someone will find out about our gold and we'll have to share it with everybody."

"Creegan's right," Rifkins said ominously, "I don't want none of you screwing this up." He was talking straight at Burke.

Burke stared back. "You think you're the foreman up top too?" he asked.

"Yes," said Rifkins. Burke squinted like a greedy toad.

"So do I," I said. As far as I was concerned, four people stealing a million bucks of gold coins need a foreman more than most groups. Kosinski growled some kind of assent and Burke was left in the position of being the last to agree.

"Sure," he mumbled. "Anything you say."

I settled back with relief. It was just as well we had gotten that item taken care of when we did. Then it occurred to me that I was thinking in terms of stealing the coins, which was not really what we were doing. It was more like taking. What no one knew was there wouldn't be missed. Would it?

"Time's up," Rifkins said. "Open the door, Burke. Everybody into the hoghouse, get showered and dressed and wait by the door for my orders."

"We don't have time to shower," Burke wailed.

"Let's not push our luck," I said quietly. "The coins have been out of our hands for half an hour already."

"Okay. No showers. But change your clothes and make it snappy."

Burke opened the door. We followed Rifkins out, into the elevator, up top and into the hoghouse, where we found Superintendent Reese and a long, lean guy in his thirties wearing a mustache, thick-rimmed glasses and a brown tweed suit. I stopped my rush through the door and stood with my mouth hanging open while Burke bumped into me and shoved me aside. Then he saw Reese and stopped too.

Superintendent Reese was one of the company overseers who was supposed to keep the job moving. His specialty, said the sign on his desk, was labor relations. He was fortyish, paunchy and a royal pain in the ass. Rumor had it he had married into the family that owned the Metropolitan Tunnel Company. The rumor was generally believed because there didn't seem any other likely explanation how someone as abrasive and incompetent as Reese could hold the job he held.

What he was doing in the hoghouse was a serious question. My immediate reaction was that somehow they'd learned about our coins and were going to take them away and fire us. From the looks on the faces of Rifkins, Burke and Kosinski, their immediate reaction was the same.

"Hello, men," Reese boomed in his hearty soup-commercial announcer's voice. He owned a grin that flickered like a faulty neon sign.

I nodded. Rifkins said, "Hello, Mr. Reese." Burke and Kosinski said nothing and moved behind Rifkins and me.

Reese looked puzzled. "How about closing the door, men? Don't want to catch cold now." Burke kicked it shut.

Reese nodded toward the lean guy in tweed. "This here's Archibald Byron. He's from the . . . the . . . one of the museums."

"The Met," Byron said in a kind of flat English accent.

"Yeah," said Reese. "The Met."

Byron smiled, showing even teeth under his mustache.

"He's got something interesting to tell you."

The four of us still huddled in a knot by the door. It was very unusual. What was a guy in tweed from the Metropolitan Museum of Art doing in the hoghouse? It scared me because museums and coins sort of go together. He couldn't know about the coins, but while he got around to telling us something "interesting," our coins would be covered by the next shift's muck.

"Actually," Byron said, "I have a question. Have any of you come across anything unusual in this tunnel? Anything different from what you've seen in other tunnels?"

I looked at Burke and Rifkins and Kosinski. They shook their heads vehemently. I said, "No, sir. Can't say that we have."

Byron looked disappointed. "Are you positive?"

"Came upon a couple of million gallons of water yesterday," said Burke with a smirk.

"Quite," said Byron. "That's why I'm here."

"Do you mind if we change while we talk?" I asked.

"Go right ahead," said Byron. "I don't wish to detain you."

We scrambled for our lockers and hauled off our clothes while Byron talked and looked uncomfortable.

"As I said, your blowout—or blow, as I've heard some of you call it—resulted in my coming here. There is some evidence that your tunnel blundered into the remains of a sunken ship." I stopped putting on my pants and stared at him. How did he know?

"What makes you think that?" I asked.

"The clean-up crew hauled out a couple of hunks of timber," said Reese.

"That's correct," said Byron. "I've had a quick look at the pieces, and they could very well have come from a ship."

"A *wooden* ship?" I asked.

"Indeed. Something lost possibly as long ago as the eighteenth century."

I glanced at Rifkins. He looked at the floor.

"Why, that's remarkable," I said. "Imagine that."

"Yeah," snarled Burke. "Well, we didn't see nothing so if you don't mind we'll be on our way."

"One moment, please," said Byron. "I know you want to get home to your wives and families. This will just take a moment." He smiled warmly. His face was weather-beaten and crinkled, as if he spent a lot of time outdoors. It wasn't the face of a guy cloistered in a museum. "I've discussed this with your employers and they've given me permission to ask you to keep a special eye out for fragments of any kind that you may come across."

"We'll do that," I said.

76

"Thank you. I've asked the same of the other crews." He paused to pick up what looked like a golf bag. From it he extracted a long metal shaft with a dish on the end. I swallowed hard and looked at Rifkins. It was a metal detector.

"This, as you probably know, is a metal detector," said Byron. "I've asked permission to go into the tunnel and see what I can find. Your company is being good about it, but they are making me wait until their lawyers can draw up some kind of a waiver of responsibility before they let me go down."

"You're going into the tunnel?" I asked.

"As soon as permission comes through."

"Ever been in air?" asked Burke.

"I beg your pardon?"

"I said you ever been in compressed air?"

"I've led a few digs in my time," Byron said with a faint smile.

"I don't think you want to go into this tunnel, Mr. Byron," I said. "It's rather dangerous."

"You go in," he said.

"I get paid for it."

"I get paid to make sure my museum gets items of historical interest. If there are pieces of a wrecked ship in your tunnel, it is my job to get them into the museum. It's a smashing piece of archeological evidence and most appropriate because it is right here in New York City."

I didn't like the sound of Byron's idea. If he went down and found some more coins, someone would start asking questions and we'd find it pretty hard to dispose of the coins we had found.

Burke said, "I don't think that doohicky there's going to be much help seeing as how the shield is all metal."

77

"I'm aware of that," Byron answered coolly. "This is a rather sophisticated instrument. It can pick metals out of a small area. All I need to do is focus it close to the area in question and flip this button." He flipped the button and the instrument, which was pointing down at my pants on the floor, emitted a shrill cry. I jumped and grabbed for my pants.

"See," said Byron. "It probably picked up your keys."

"Right." I pretended to look into the pocket. "Keys."

Byron chuckled, and tailed his detector on Burke. When he turned it on it shrieked again.

"Keys," said Burke.

Byron moved it to Burke's other pocket. It shrieked.

"What's that?" asked Byron.

"How the hell should I know?" Burke snapped.

"Take a look," said Reese. Burke looked panicky.

"It's your knife, isn't it?" I asked him.

"What? Yeah, right. My knife."

Byron glanced sharply from one to the other. He said nothing for a moment and I had the feeling he was damned bright and was tumbling to something. He said, "The people of the City of New York have a right to share the treasures of their city, be they paintings in a museum or artifacts not yet displayed. It would be unfair to ... prevent ... such artifacts from reaching their attention."

I nodded vigorously.

Byron gazed at Burke with a look that seemed to penetrate his eyes and delve deep into his soul. Burke glared back, but then I could almost see the chips on his shoulders turn into sawdust. He rumbled something deep in his chest, shuffled his feet, and looked away.

Triumph flickered over Byron's face. The naked light

bulb hanging overhead glinted knowingly off his glasses as he inspected each of our faces in turn. I started to panic, knowing we were losing control of the situation. I opened my mouth, but Byron spoke first.

"Men," he said crisply. "My instincts tell me you're hiding something."

I tried to look indignant.

"Bull," mumbled Burke.

Rifkins's face jerked spasmodically. Kosinski looked sternly uncomfortable, and Reese glared like a suspicious pig.

Byron suddenly switched on the detector and swept it past us. At each front pocket the instrument shrieked in a shrill voice that seemed to say, "Gold coins, gold coins, gold coins."

Reese came alert, his face turning mean. "What are you guys up to?" he asked.

No one answered.

Reese snapped, "Everything in the tunnel belongs to the Metropolitan Tunnel Company. You can't take anything out."

"Even the mud?" asked Burke.

"That's right, Burke," Reese snapped back. "We get a good price for landfill." He glared at us. "Empty your pockets, all of you." Byron watched, a contemptuous curl playing over his mouth.

Rifkins automatically reached for his pocket, his face a mixture of guilt and fear. I grabbed his arm. "You can't make us empty our pockets."

"I can too," said Reese. "Empty them or get off the job."

That threat hung in the air for several seconds. Keeping my grip on Rifkins's arm, I turned toward the back of the room, and whispered to Burke, "Just keep yelling. I'll get the steward." Burke nodded and started yelling. I yanked Rifkins away with me and muttered, "Slip me your coins."

He nodded gratefully. Being a company man, the foreman would sooner or later have to empty his pockets. I grabbed the phone, called the office and asked for the shop steward. I explained that an injustice was being done. He was at the door two seconds after I'd put down the phone.

"O.K.," I said to Burke. "Stop yelling." He was questioning the birthright of Reese and Byron. He stopped in fits and jerks, a few choice epithets squeezing out in the end.

The shop steward slammed the door emphatically. His face gleamed with readiness for battle.

Bends, or caisson disease, as I've mentioned, happens when a man returns from high air pressure too quickly. Paul Kavanaugh, the shop steward, was a victim of bends. His hands were gnarled and twisted and he walked with a limp. He got the bends about fifty years ago because the company he was working for didn't like to pay its men for too much time in the decompression chamber. It saved them a few bucks at the time. Kavanaugh, too crippled to work, helped organize a union for sandhogs and over the years exacted a pretty heavy return for his disability. The sandhogs in Local 147 of the Miners, Drillers and Blasters were the main recipients.

Kavanaugh, who must have been hitting eighty but had more fire in his boiler than John L. Lewis on his best day, grinned viciously, hobbled over to Reese and looked him straight in the eye.

"Your demands are unreasonable, unjust and impossible." Then he hobbled over to me and asked, "What does he want?"

"He says we have to empty our pockets or we're fired."

"He does, does he?" Kavanaugh cackled evilly. He turned back to Reese, taking in Archibald Byron with a quick look of distaste.

"You would be firing men for demanding their rights as free citizens and honest laborers?"

Reese purpled. "Hold on, Kavanaugh, this has nothing to do with you."

Kavanaugh said, "You'd be depriving the working man of his right to a living?"

"That has nothing to do with it."

"You'd be threatening union men with arbitrary dismissal?"

"Excuse me, sir," said Byron. Kavanaugh reacted to the English accent with a horrified cock of his scrawny head.

"And who would you be?" he asked with a sneer.

"Archibald Byron of the Metropolitan Museum of Art."

"What, Mr. Archibald Byron of the Metropolitan Museum of Art, would you be doing in a hoghouse?"

Byron said with elaborate patience, "Mr. Reese and I have reason to believe these men took valuable artifacts from the tunnel. All we want is to see those artifacts in their proper depository."

Kavanaugh blinked.

Reese said, "These guys stole stuff from the tunnel."

Kavanaugh stiffened. "Would you be saying," he asked very softly, "that the brothers of One Forty-seven are thieves?"

"If they took stuff from the tunnel then they're thieves," Reese snapped.

Kavanaugh stared for a long time. The room went silent. The old shop steward hobbled to the phone, painfully dialed the office, and said, "Strike."

Chapter 11

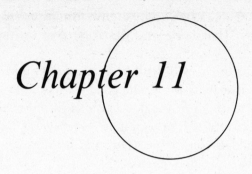

"You can't," howled Reese.

Old Kavanaugh gently replaced the phone in its cradle. His eyes shined. "We're going out, boys. It'll be a long one."

"Wait," yelled Reese. "We can talk. Man to man. Management to labor. We'll work it out."

Kavanaugh ignored him. He rubbed his crippled fingers and spoke to us, the sandhogs, with a reverent quaver. "I'll leave you now, boys. We've got to clear the tunnel. Report here in the morning for picket duty. I've a busy night ahead with the other unions."

"Please," said Reese. "Not all of them. Let's talk this out before it goes too far."

"It has gone far too far already, Mr. Reese. Management will learn someday, I hope, that labor is not to be trifled with like defenseless children. We have our strengths, sir. We have teeth."

"You're going crazy, you old fool," Reese was responding to the situation with typical intelligence. Kavanaugh smiled vaguely, apparently unruffled. But he spoke coldly. "That'll cost you, Mr. Reese. Aye. Cost you plenty."

I exchanged looks with Rifkins. Reese wasn't that far off about Kavanaugh, for all the good it would do him. Kavanaugh reached for the doorknob. "I would be advising you, Mr. Reese, that you don't belong here. Take Mr. Archibald Byron of the Metropolitan Museum of Art and leave these men in peace."

For once, Reese showed sense. Curtly nodding at Byron, he stormed past Kavanaugh. Byron hurriedly packed his metal detector and followed after him. Kavanaugh winked broadly and went in their wake.

"Now we've done it," said Rifkins. "The company's going to be pretty upset with a strike on top of a blow."

"Screw 'em," said Burke.

"The union isn't going to be exactly thrilled either," I said. Things had been going well on the Long Island Railroad Tunnel, plenty of work, decent benefits and cordial union-management relations. It was the wrong time for a strike.

"Them too," said Burke.

"We're wasting time here," said Kosinski. "Let's get our gold."

We finished changing and left the hoghouse.

It was the most beautiful night I had ever seen. Cold, sharp, clean air, black on top and pricked with stars, it was everything the tunnel wasn't.

"There's the barge," Burke hissed excitedly.

"Don't point," Rifkins snapped. Burke retracted his arm and hopped about agitatedly. We stood just outside the hoghouse door. The elevator building loomed like a tremendous brick placed on end. Beyond the elevator was the East River. Upstream, two hundred yards, was the barge in question. Surreptitiously we inspected it. A trillion lighted Manhattan windows across the river provided a backdrop for the bridges to our left and right. Down near the Williamsburg span a lone tug with red and green and white running lights moved upriver. Behind us was the staging area for tunnel materials, the parking lot and the gate that opened onto the road that went off Welfare Island to Queens.

The gate. Jeannie. She said she'd pick me up, which meant she was probably waiting already. I nudged Rifkins.

"Hey. Somebody's waiting for me. I better tell her I'll be awhile."

"Let her wait," Burke said. "Does 'em good."

"I don't think we want her asking the guard what happened to me. If he checks up . . ."

"Get over there and tell her," Rifkins snapped. "Hurry it up." I turned to run. "Wait. See that shed? Meet us there." He pointed out a shed used for storing equipment about halfway between us and the barge. I said I would. Rifkins warned me not to be seen going there. I said I'd be careful and ran off in search of Jeannie. When I reached the gate and looked back, Rifkins, Burke and Kosinski were out of sight.

The gate guard was in his shed and it occurred to me that it would be better in case something went wrong if he didn't remember me going out and coming back a few minutes later. I spotted Jeannie's car and made my way along the chain link fence until I was as near to it as I could get. The overhead lighting in the project area was spotty, giving me some shadows to stick to. Crouching in one, I called Jeannie's name. Her square-nosed car was about twenty feet away, and she didn't answer.

I lofted a handful of gravel over the fence and onto the roof of her car. That got her. The door flew open and she and Howard emerged together, Jeannie saying, "What the hell?" and Howard growling like he meant it.

"Over here," I called.

"Who the . . . ?"

"It's me, Jeannie. Dick," I whispered.

In the shadowy light I couldn't make out her face clearly enough to see what she was thinking. I called again and she understood. At least she shoved Howard back into the car and closed the door. Then she inspected the roof for scratches and sauntered over.

"What's with you?" she asked. "Won't they let you out?"

I gripped the fence with both hands and whispered rapidly. "Quiet. Listen." She seemed to see I meant it, because her puzzled expression vanished. She touched my fingers through the fence and said, "I'm listening."

"We found more gold coins," I said. "I don't have time to explain. But if you can, wait here and I'll be back as soon as we get the stuff out."

Jeannie said, "If you don't have time don't waste it here. I'll wait. Just be careful whatever. O.K.?"

"O.K. See you." I loped away into the night, approaching the supply shed in a broad circle. Once there, I saw no one, but as I passed the door a hand reached out and dragged me inside. It was Rifkins.

"Anybody see you?"

"No."

"Good. Here's your shovel." He handed me a shovel. I took it with distaste until I noticed everyone had one. Things were getting better already. Or so I thought until I noticed the glum looks on their faces. Burke and Kosinski were skulking by the window. Rifkins looked nervous and worried. I asked what was wrong.

"Everything," snarled Burke. I stepped to the window and looked out.

"There's a guy on the barge," Rifkins said from behind me.

"I see that."

"And too much light."

"We figured there would be."

"We also figured we'd steal a truck and drive the stuff out," Rifkins replied. "See any trucks?"

"Not from here."

"There is one," Burke said.

"Only thing is," Rifkins continued, "it's parked next to the main office, and the project manager is leaning on its front fender talking to the chief engineer."

"Sounds like a problem."

"This is a very funny kid," Burke observed harshly.

"My friend is sitting in her car right outside the fence," I said. "We'll use that."

"And how do we get to the fence?" Rifkins asked.

I looked around. It was very simple. "How about a couple of these wheelbarrows?" No one said anything. I looked out the window again. "See there?" I asked. "Past the barge. We'll just circle around along the edge of the fence all the way to there." I pointed to a spot just within our angle of vision. "The car isn't more than a few yards beyond that."

"What about the fence?" asked Rifkins.

"Find some wirecutters. There must be some in here someplace."

"Somebody'll spot the hole."

"By the time they do we'll be long gone. Besides, somebody's always breaking in here stealing things. They'll think that's what it was."

"You don't have much respect for property, do you?"

I turned to Rifkins and gave him a look. Off the job he wasn't quite the awesome figure he was on the job. He glared angrily, but turned away. Burke chuckled evilly.

"O.K., smart guy," Rifkins said. "So we wheelbarrow the stuff into your broad's car. What about the guy on the barge and the lights? Huh?"

I looked back out the window. Kosinski stirred uneasily, wetting his lips. Burke kept his face pressed to the glass. He left twin vapor trails under his nose. Big lamps on top of temporary wooden poles spotted the area with bright light. The wires ran overhead, connecting them. Short of climbing a pole right under the glare of a light, there didn't seem to be a way of cutting them. I'd assumed we could just slice into the offending wires running up the pole, but they were beyond reach.

"How you going to cut the wires?" Rifkins asked petulantly. "You got the answers." I ignored him and kept looking, thinking that the leadership of the group had shifted subtly in my direction.

Therefore, when I suddenly saw the answer to the lighting problem, I hesitated to speak. I wasn't sure I was interested in leading the rest of the guys anywhere. I'd spent all my working days listening to other people's orders. That's a nice and simple way of living. All you have to do is what you're told and as long as you make it clear you have limits, you can coast along with no worries. I thought if I waited awhile someone else, Rifkins probably, would see the answer. So I kept my mouth shut and continued looking out the window.

"See," Rifkins asked suddenly, "there's no way. They'll spot us as soon as we get on the barge."

"I want my gold," Burke whined. "I want it."

"Well, you're not going to get it," Rifkins said disgustedly, "because we listened to Creegan's damned fool idea about sending the stuff out on the battleship."

"Yeah, it's Creegan's fault."

"There was no other way," Kosinski rumbled deep in his chest.

I was beginning to like Kosinski very much. I'd also decided it was up to me to get things moving.

"All right. Who's an electrician?"

"What?"

"Which one of you guys can do a simple wiring job?"

They stared around at each other blankly. *I* didn't know a damned thing about electricity, but we needed someone who did and I'd hoped that among the three of them there was an amateur electrical worker.

"Nobody?" I asked.

"What do you want wired?" It was Kosinski. Of course.

"Come over here," I said, leading a puzzled threesome to a big grey metal box on the wall, out of which ran dozens of wires. "Believe it or not," I said, "the wires from the spotlights run right into this building." I glanced around, forcing my face to remain neutral. I was ready to crack up when Rifkins ran to the window and shuffled back with a sheepish look. "Which means," I continued after a moment's respectful and embarrassed silence, "that we can probably just turn the lights off with a switch. Right?"

They nodded. "Trouble is, somebody else can turn them right back on. So if Kosinski can figure out a way to keep them from being turned back on without making it look too obvious, we can go out there and get our gold."

Kosinski opened the door on the box and peered in. Rifkins warned him not to electrocute himself. Kosinski ignored him and poked around with his finger. After a few minutes he said he had found what he needed and asked which lights I wanted out. He and I went back to window and studied the scene. We agreed that we'd have good cover if the two lights nearest the barge and five more along the fence were put out. Then we went back to the box.

Kosinski looked at me. "Say when."

"Wait," Rifkins said. "What about the guy on the barge?"

"He'll leave when the lights don't come back on."

"And what if he don't?" asked Burke.

I didn't know the answer to that one. Neither, it seemed, did anyone else. I said, "When the lights don't come back on, why would he sit around? He'll be glad for an excuse to get out of the cold."

Rifkins seemed to be making a tremendous effort not to look doubtful. I could tell by the look on his face that he, like me, was hoping that the man would disappear just because we wanted him to. Still, I honestly couldn't imagine a working guy hanging around that barge in the dark when he could get inside someplace warm. I hoped.

Finally, when no one said anything more, I suggested that we get a couple of wheelbarrows and begin. Rifkins and Burke placed two big ones, the kind with the big inflated tire, by the door. Kosinski and I waited by the box.

"O.K.," Rifkins said. "As soon as the lights go out, follow us to the barge. But look out for that guy. Me and Burke'll circle around so we don't run into him."

I went to the window. Things seemed normal. I hurried back to Kosinski. "O.K.?"

"When?"

"Don't you need wire and tools?"

"Circuit breakers," he said. "I'll bend them a little so they can't go back in. When?"

"When."

Kosinski went click, click, click. I ran to the window. The barge was gone in the dark. No one would spot us now. Our only problem would be finding the thing.

"Good," I said to Kosinski. He was busy bending circuit breakers. Then he went click again, and the shed went dark. "Slow them up," he explained, as we stumbled toward the door.

Outside, there was light behind us toward the hoghouse and the office. But toward the barge was black as the river. Ahead I heard Rifkins and Burke madly wheelbarrowing along. Kosinski and I trotted after them.

We circled east, away from the river, until we were nearly in line with the barge. I found Burke and Rifkins. Already my eyes were accustomed to the dark, and the light from the city made it possible to distinguish various shapes and forms, including that of the barge resting at the river bank.

The guy on the barge was yelling something about lights. After a few minutes he gave up. But none of us saw him leave. A desperately whispered conversation among us ended when no one was able to guarantee the guy wasn't there.

"Give him some time," I said. "He'll get cold."

"I'm cold already," Burke said.

The combination of the excitement and my sheep kept me warm, in fact sweating. I kept staring at the bulky shape of the barge but I couldn't see the man. I would have thought he would be silhouetted against the Manhattan lights.

It was so quiet where we were, you could hear the traffic on the F.D.R. Drive across the river and the muffled beat of a tugboat engine as she passed under the Fifty-ninth Street Bridge, a quarter-mile downstream from us. The bridge was beginning to bother me, because its lights penetrated the area we'd darkened. After a few more minutes, I was about to run closer for a better look when suddenly Burke said, "There he is."

And there he was, standing up on top of the barge, energetically waving a flashlight.

"What the hell's he doing?" Burke asked.

"What's he waving that light at?" I asked.

"He's signaling somebody," said Rifkins.

"Who?"

"How the hell am I supposed to know—Oh Christ, look at that."

We were already looking.

The man with the flashlight turned it off. He didn't need it anymore, because the barge was suddenly illuminated as bright as day by the tremendous searchlight on the tugboat that was steaming directly at it.

"He's going to hit the barge," Burke yelled.

Indeed, the tug would have hit the barge had it not slowed and wheeled smartly about at the last moment, coming to rest alongside. A couple of men jumped from the tug to the barge, tugging heavy lines after them. Then, as we watched in sick fascination, they drew the lines tight. The mound of muck on the barge obscured what they were doing, but it didn't take too much imagination to realize they were tying the two craft together.

The guy with the flashlight clambered off the barge. The line tuggers hopped back on the tug. Then the guy with the flashlight untied the ropes that held the barge to the dock. The tug blew one sharp blast of whistle. The spotlight was extinguished. The tug engine beat heavily.

We watched the tugboat pull away from the dock.

We watched the barge go with it.

Chapter 12

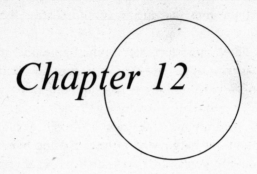

The tug and our barge moved into the center of the river.

A plaintive howl broke our stunned silence. "But that's *our* gold." It was Burke. When the tug reached midstream, it continued its graceful sweep until it was heading back downriver from whence it came.

"But. But."

"Where's he going?" Rifkins asked.

No one answered. It hardly mattered where he was going because none of us had thought to bring a boat. Had we, it would have been a simple matter to leap into it, start its engine or engines and take off in stern pursuit. Instead, we stood there in the dark on Welfare Island with our shovels and our wirecutter and wheelbarrows and cursed viciously.

Anger began to burn inside me, directed at the louts on

the tugboat who were hauling a million dollars they didn't even know about to an undisclosed location. Some about-to-be-violated marsh somewhere would be the recipient of the most expensive landfill since Atlantis went under.

But where? Where were they taking the stuff? Who could we ask? Someone must know. Excuse me, sir, but after shoveling muck for seven years in tunnels all over the world I was suddenly wondering where the muck goes and thought perhaps you could tell me. A likely question.

The tug and our barge were already passing beneath the Fifty-ninth Street Bridge. I stared after it. In doing so I noticed the cars on the F.D.R. Drive in Manhattan and wondered how stupid four people could be.

"We can follow him," I yelled. "Come on. We'll chase him down the Drive. Hurry." I was already running and had gotten halfway to the gate when Rifkins caught up and grabbed my shoulder.

"Hold on, Creegan. We can't just come running out of the dark. Head for the hoghouse. We'll walk out from there."

"You're right, but hurry. We have to get off this silly island and over the bridge."

"I know." We ran next to each other toward the hoghouse. When we were back in the light, we slowed, let Kosinski and Burke catch up, and then sauntered casually past the project manager and the chief engineer, still engrossed in their blueprints and seemingly oblivious of the cold.

The four of us continued across the site and out the gate, waving good night to the guard in his shack. Then we strolled rapidly across the parking lot toward Jeannie's Rollswagen (or Volksroyce).

Jeannie rolled down her window and said hi to me and looked up at the four of us staring down at her car as though we were considering a Christmas present for a small child.

"I hope you're not planning on doing what it looks like you're planning on doing," she said.

"We are," I said, "if you don't mind."

"Where are we going?"

"Down the F.D.R. Rapidly." I went around the other side, opened the door and said to my companions, "Hop in the back."

They stared at each other and at the car. Still, crowding was a minor concern at that point. Burke ran around to my side and leaped in the back. Then he yelled and leaped back out, his face contorted with shock. *What's that?*

I looked in. "That's Howard. Be nice to him and he'll be nice to you. Get in."

"Not me."

I turned to Rifkins, then thought better of it. "Kosinski. You go in first. He won't hurt you." Kosinski bent down and looked inside, paused a second and extended his hand, fingers curled inward. "Hello," he said. Howard glared, then tentatively licked his knuckles.

"Move over, Howard," Jeannie said impatiently. "Just shove him over," she told Kosinski.

"That's O.K., Miss," Kosinski mumbled and crammed his six feet five inches onto the seat. Howard retreated reluctantly under Jeannie's urging.

"O.K.," I said to Burke. "Get in."

"No way."

"Rifkins?"

Rifkins climbed in laboriously. I motioned Burke after him.

"Where?" he asked. Good question. Howard, Kosinski and Rifkins were a carful unto themselves. I told them to move over. Rifkins pushed against Kosinski, who pushed against Howard, who started making irritated noises. Eventually we squeezed enough room for about half of Burke. He rested the other half gingerly on Rifkins's lap. I pushed the front seat back down, noticed the tires were more oval than round and climbed in.

"We have to chase a tugboat down the East River," I said to Jeannie. She started the engine and headed slowly out of the potholed parking lot. "He has a bit of a head start on us," I added.

"He'll have more of a head start if I break an axle getting out of here," she replied. I shut my mouth.

As we crossed the bridge into Queens, Jeannie said, "Before you introduce me to your friends, could you tell me why we have to chase a tugboat down the East River?"

"I'll introduce you first. It's easier." I turned around and raised my voice over the straining engine. "This is Kosinski, next to Howard. Then our foreman Rifkins in the middle and then Burke. Everybody, this is my friend Jeannie."

"Hello, everybody," Jeannie called over her shoulder. "Nice to meet you."

A shy and mumbled chorus of yeahs drifted up from the back seat. I faced front.

"Why are we chasing a tugboat?" Jeannie pulled onto the Fifty-ninth Street Bridge. I tried to calculate how far down the river the tug would be by now. It seemed like a long time since he'd left the dock with our barge. But when I reviewed in my mind what we had done, I realized he had at most a six- or seven-minute lead.

"I told you about finding more coins," I said.

"Yes?"

"We found eighteen hundred and forty-seven."

Jeannie turned to me wide-eyed. "How much did you say yours were worth?"

"That's right," I said. "We found about a million dollars worth. Maybe more."

"What's my cut for chasing the tugboat?"

"Union scale."

"Thanks. What happened to the coins?"

"We had to send them out of the tunnel with the mud. We figured on getting them off the barge the mud is dumped on."

"Don't tell me a tugboat took the barge?"

"If I didn't I'd be keeping things from you."

"Where's the tug going?"

"Down the river. Slow down." We were in the middle of the bridge, high over the East River. "Anybody see him?" I yelled. As we were heading west and the tug was heading south, he would be somewhere to our left. Jeannie was between me and the left front window. Howard obscured most of the rear left window. I couldn't see anything moving on the river. The bridge stanchions were whipping by. We'd be off the thing soon. I told Jeannie to stop.

"We're in the middle of the bridge."

"I know. Stop."

She muttered something, looked in the rear-view mirror, where undoubtedly all she saw was Rifkins's nervous countenance, and applied the brakes.

"I hope nothing is coming," she said. She flipped on her flashers and hunched down to peer into her side-view mirror. I tried to look around her head and when that proved futile opened my door and stepped out, nearly putting the end to a cab driver's night. He waved an apolitical clenched fist. I pressed against the Rollswagen and tried to be thin.

When he was past I ran around the car and looked across the eastbound traffic lanes. The black water reflected lights from both sides. A gargantuan Pepsi sign, perhaps the largest one in the universe, painted acres of the surface blood red. Squinting, I commenced a scan sweep of the river, starting at the Williamsburg Bridge far in the distance. He couldn't have gotten farther than that.

It looked like the bastard had sunk. Served him right.

"See anything?" Jeannie called.

"No. He's—wait. Yes. There along the shore. After him."

"Why don't you get back in the car first?"

I ran back around and climbed in just ahead of a tremendous fuel tanker. "Go!" I yelled. Jeannie went. But with four sandhogs, one working actress, and Howard, the Rollswagen went reluctantly. I kept my eye on the tug until we left the bridge. Then, in order to get onto the F.D.R. Drive, we had to enter city streets and wait interminably at two red lights, during which time we were out of sight of the river.

Back on the F.D.R., we found ourselves under the overhang that keeps Sutton Place above the traffic. The retaining walls and the three northbound lanes between us and the water made it difficult to see the river.

I suggested to Jeannie that we go faster. She suggested I shut up. Rifkins told Burke to get his hand off his leg. Burke snapped that Rifkins and Kosinski should move over. They did. Howard moaned. Kosinski patted his massive head to calm him but Howard wasn't buying any. He moaned some more and began thrashing around as much as his dwindling allotment of space permitted.

"Behave yourself, Howard," Jeannie said over her shoulder.

"Yeah," I said, "just quiet down, Howard." I was getting irritable.

"Leave him alone," Jeannie commanded. She was too, it seemed. Then we passed under the overhang that keeps the United Nations from blocking the highway, and again visibility was checked.

Howard's moans were sounding awesomely like growls.

"He's getting mad," Burke said shrilly. "What happens then?" I turned around. Burke looked terrified.

"Why don't you make friends with him?" I suggested. "He's upset because the back seat is his. That's all. He doesn't hate you or anything."

Burke blinked. "You think so?"

The Rollswagen suddenly hit an ice patch and went into a three-quarters skid. Jeannie swore and steered out of it. Her lips were pressed tightly. Her eyes narrowed. Then she stomped the accelerator to the floor. Gradually the car went faster.

"Go on," I said to Burke. "Give him a little rub behind the ears. He'll love you."

"I don't know," Burke said apprehensively.

"Pat him, already," Rifkins snarled. "You're the reason he's pissed off." He looked up at the rear-view mirror. "Oh, sorry, Miss."

"Don't pay it any mind," Jeannie said. Her hands were clenched on the wheel. The speedometer said we were doing seventy, which was twenty-five more than the signs on the road, and, in my opinion at least, thirty more than the icy pavement called for.

I searched in vain for the tug. The river looked empty again. It must have been one or two in the morning. Even the F.D.R. traffic was light.

"I'm going to do it now," Burke said.

"Good," said Rifkins.

"Don't scare him," said Kosinski. I turned around to watch with one eye. The other searched the river. Burke put a brave smile on his face and reached, suddenly, with his right hand. There followed in quick-time a roar, a yelp and a sharp click. The first was Howard, the second Burke, and the third Howard's incisors. Kosinski had one arm under Howard's neck, holding him back, and the other behind him, stroking his ears, into which he murmured soothing noises. Howard listened and relaxed. Burke slumped white-faced in his corner and nodded weakly when Jeannie assured him that Howard wouldn't bite.

"Where's the tug?" Rifkins asked.

"I can't find it."

"You can't lose an eighty-foot tug and a hundred-foot barge."

"Yeah," said everyone, glumly, as we passed under the Williamsburg Bridge. The river widened into the spur that went off into the Brooklyn Navy Yard.

"Do you think he crossed over?" Jeannie asked.

"We would have seen him out in the middle. He's hugging the shore."

When we passed in quick succession under the Manhattan Bridge and the Brooklyn Bridge I began to have doubts. "We've come too far," I said, as the Seaport Museum whipped past. Shortly after that the road dropped down to water level, revealing an empty river and the Upper New York Bay. Jeannie pulled off the F.D.R. and onto South Street.

"Where you going?"

"Downtown heliport. We can see more from the pier."

I nodded dejectedly.

"We lost him," Burke moaned. "All our gold. My million bucks. Gone."

"Quarter million," I said reflexively.

Jeannie squealed the Rollswagen into the heliport through a driveway plastered with no admittance signs and out onto the end of the pier. I jumped out and stared into the darkness. Upriver was nothing. Some lights moved out in the bay. Jeannie walked up to me.

"See anything?"

"Nothing, dammit."

"What's out there?" she asked, pointing at the moving lights.

"Freighters, I hope. If the tug's there, we'll never find him."

Howard was suddenly next to her. She dropped her hand to his head and said to me, "I'm sorry, Hog. I really am."

"You did the best you could," I answered. "If you hadn't been there we wouldn't have had a chance. Lousy luck."

Burke and Rifkins and Kosinski came up to us. Burke was cursing and moaning and complaining and blaming me for the whole thing. I wasn't in the mood, so I reminded him that if it hadn't been for me he wouldn't have found the gold in the first place. He replied that if it wasn't for my dumb idea about sending it out in the battleship we wouldn't have lost it. I didn't have the energy to argue.

It was cold out on the pier. Tremendous gusts of wind came off the bay. Jeannie put her arm into mine and rested her head on my shoulder. She whispered that we should drop Burke and Rifkins and Kosinski someplace and go out for a late dinner. I was about to agree when a guy came running up yelling that we were trespassing on private property and we shouldn't have driven our car out on the pier and that the helicopters weren't running anymore that night.

We all turned and stared at him. He looked us over, apparently decided we weren't about to be paying customers and ordered us off the pier. As we headed for the car Jeannie told him we thought we had seen a helicopter crash into the river and that's why we drove out onto his private property.

"Where?" he asked.

Burke and Rifkins and Kosinski and Howard had already wedged themselves back in the car. "There," Jeannie said, pointing generally southward, and climbed in. I followed and the guy trotted alongside screaming questions until Jeannie stepped on it and left him behind.

"He musta turned off," Kosinski suddenly said from the back.

"Who?"

"The tugboat. He must of stopped someplace along the way where we couldn't see him."

"We'll never find him," Burke said.

Chapter 13

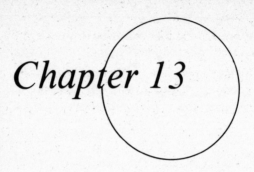

The next day, while Burke and Kosinski manned a picket line, and Rifkins squirmed through management meetings, I went to the South Street Seaport Museum.

I walked out on the pier, past a partially restored four-master, a Gloucesterman fishing boat, a Hudson River sidewheeler, a display of painted figureheads, and a barrel requesting contributions, to which I contributed, all the way to the end, where I could watch the East River.

I was looking for tugboats.

I saw a number of them while I shivered in the weak morning sun. The first one hauled barges of trap rock upstream from the offshore mines. It hugged the right side of the channel to allow room for another towing garbage downstream. Three of them pushed a gleaming white Norwegian freighter toward a berth on the Brooklyn shore. Several more came by pushing oilers. Others hurried by alone like executives who'd missed their early train.

None stopped at the pier or even came close enough to hail.

When I got hungry around noon I had lunch at the Sketch Pad, which Jeannie says is the last bar in New York that's still like the bars in the Village used to be in Kerouac's time.

Then I walked down to the Battery, hoping for better luck. A fireboat and some Coast Guard launches passed close to the shore, but the only tugs I saw were way out, nudging cruise ships toward the Narrows.

I gave up after an hour, had some coffee, and headed uptown for another try. This time I chose the Morton Street Pier, which juts out into the Hudson like a Greenwich Village version of Coney Island.

I figured the only way we would ever find where our bargeload of coins went would be to find the tug that had hauled it away. But I was leery of asking anyone at the job or from the tug companies, because it might look suspicious, especially since the museum was onto our find, and the tunnel company believed that we had taken something of value. It wouldn't take too much intelligence on their part to figure we'd slipped out a whole load of stuff, even if they didn't know precisely what it was. I had the feeling that Archibald Byron had a pretty fair idea of what we had taken. He would reason that a bunch of sandhogs wouldn't bother stealing wooden timbers. If he knew anything about the history of the East River, and it seemed likely he would, he would damned sure know about Jonathan Ludlum's sunken gold ship. So I had to track the barge without leaving any tracks of my own.

I hoped to find a tied-up tug and get into a conversation with the crewmen and find out what tug company had the towing contract for our tunnel. Then, with luck, I'd find a tug from *that* company, and eventually find the name of the tug that took our barge. Then I'd find that tug and ask where they had dumped the mud. Presumably, it was being used for landfill. I didn't even want to consider the possibility that it had been dumped underwater someplace. We'd have a hard enough time as it was locating our coins in the tremendous amount of mud the barge carried.

It was a freezing cold day, though brilliantly sunny, and I had the pier to myself, except for the occasional insane bicyclist who'd tick, tick, tick, out to the end where I sat, and then quickly tick, tick, tick, back out of the wind. I wrapped the sheep around me and scanned the water through my sunglasses.

I'd been there an hour, and was considering going someplace for hot coffee, when a tug veered in from the middle of the river. He came close, but stopped at the next pier down, and fastened onto an oiler that was snubbed alongside a tiny passenger liner.

I started to get to my feet, hoping to run down the pier into the shore and out onto the next pier, when I realized that even if I got there in time I'd still have to get onto the liner. That didn't seem very likely, so I slumped back on my bench. A few minutes later, the tug left with the oiler. I waited gloomily. There had to be a better way.

Another tug, long, but lower than the other, came into view from the south. It drew my interest because it was hugging the line of the outstretched piers as if it was about to land. I stood, ready to start running to whatever pier it was going to.

Someone appeared on the bow and grabbed a line. The tug, murky blue and off-green paint scaling from the sides, turned in to the south side of the Morton Street Pier about a hundred feet from me in the lee of the north wind, and nosed its bow against the crumbling pilings. I got up and walked over.

The bulkily clad guy on the bow waved to the pilot. Just as I reached the spot where it had been, it pulled back until a couple of dozen feet of water showed between it and me.

Then it edged forward again, striking the pier a few yards down. The guy with the rope skillfully looped it around a cleat on the dock, then took a turn around his own cleat. The uneven beat of the engine quickened, the tug pulled back against the line and, with a loud crack, the cleat pulled out of the Morton Street Pier and splashed into the water.

The guy yanked the line until the broken-off cleat reached the surface; then, checking to make sure he had a secure hold on the thing, he pulled it hand over hand onto the deck, where it dropped with a heavy clunk. Where it had resided on the pier was a splintered piece of rotten piling with lots of holes in it.

Seeing my chance to strike up a conversation, I called, "Throw me line, I'll tie you to something more solid."

"That's O.K. We'll manage." His face was nearly hidden in the fur of his parka. He untangled his line and signaled the pilot. The tug approached the pier, and again, with a deft wrist-flick, the guy on the bow got a double loop around another big cleat.

The tug backed off, testing its grip. The cleat creaked,

but didn't budge. The engine throbbed louder than before. Water boiled up under the hull and eddied around the pilings. Still hoping to make conversation, I called, "Looks like you got a good one this time."

"Yeah," said the guy on the bow. He signaled the pilot and black smoke poured from the funnel as the engine wound up to what sounded like half-power. The cleat began to pull from the wood. It seemed to me that the tug crew was overdoing the matter of testing their mooring. No force other than a hurricane could approximate the pull they were already exerting on the cleat.

Suddenly the pilot cut a sharp, short blast on his horn and pointed frantically from the wheel house. The crewman and I looked toward the street. Two cops were strolling through the entry to the pier. The engine died to a murmur and the tug nudged the piling. The crewman flipped the line off the cleat they'd been testing and tried to yank it aboard, but it tangled on a bunch of rusty spikes.

"Come on," yelled the pilot, sticking his head out the side window.

"It's stuck," said the crewman. He looked up at me. "Hey, kid, untangle that thing." I knelt down and worked the line loose. The crewman hauled it up and the engine beat changed as the pilot started to back off. "Thanks, kid," the guy yelled as he turned toward the stern.

On impulse, I ran forward and leaped the four or five feet of black water. I landed on the deck, lost my balance and fell forward on my face.

"What the hell?" said the guy.

"I hope you don't mind," I said as I stood up, "but I've got to talk to you."

"You a cop?"

"No."

"Coast Guard?"

"No."

"Harbor patrol?"

"No."

"Private security guard?"

The deck heeled as the pilot spun his wheel and sent the boat forward in a sharp circle. We were midway between the two piers and heading fast for the open river. The cops were standing where I had been, puzzled expressions on their faces.

"I'm not anything to do with law," I said. "I just want to ask some questions."

The guy looked at me for a moment. Even close up, I could hardly see his face because the parka hood covered it. What I could see was seamed and brown. He spoke with the faintest hint of a Southern drawl. The tug reached open water and the wind came cutting down out of the north to sweep the deck like frozen razor blades.

"Come on in the warm," he said. I followed him up the ladder to the wheel house. The pilot spun the wheel until we were heading south. Then, in heavy Scandinavian tones, he asked me what the hell I was doing on his boat. The deck hand said I wanted to ask some questions.

"What's your name?"

"Dick Creegan."

"I'm Dave Ericsson. This here's Travis Jones." I shook hands with both men. Ericsson opened a voice pipe and yelled, "Coffee."

A voice came back sharply. "Take your choice. Coffee or engines."

"I'll get it," said Jones, wearily.

Ericsson said, "Thanks a lot," into the voice pipe and capped it, cutting off some heartfelt profanity.

"Better give me a hand carrying it up," Jones said to me.

"Sure," I said, though I was reluctant to leave the magnificent view of the harbor the wheel house offered. I followed Jones down the ladder and into a bunk room with a galley at one end. The bunks and most of the deck were buried under piles of dock cleats similar to the one that had pulled loose from the Morton Street Pier.

"How you want your coffee?"

"Black."

"Stick your head down there," he said, pointing at the entrance to the engine room, "and see if he wants any." I looked in and yelled to a guy who was sitting on another pile of cleats. "Want coffee?"

"Who are you?"

"Just visiting."

"Yeah, I want coffee."

"He wants coffee," I told Jones.

"Tell him to get lost," Jones said cheerfully.

"I think you better tell him," I said.

Jones split his dark face with crooked white teeth. "Just this once, we'll let him have the coffee." He mixed milk and sugar into a steaming mug and carried it down to the engineer. Then we carried three cups up to the wheel house.

"Thanks very much," I said. "Cold as a bastard."

"What you want to know?"

"I'm trying to locate a tugboat."

"That you've done, kid. What you want towed?"

"Nothing. I'm looking for a particular boat."

Ericsson glanced over from the wheel, disappointment

in his face. "What's wrong with this boat? We'll give you a good price."

"It isn't that," I said. "I'm trying to locate a boat that towed a certain barge last night."

"Why?"

I had thought about that question ahead of time. People were sure to ask it. I'd decided to play it by ear. Now that it was asked, my ear wasn't being very helpful. Jones and Ericsson looked at me curiously.

"I can't really say," I said, lamely. "It's sort of private."

"Just wondering," said Jones. "Doesn't matter."

"Thanks. I was hoping that you might be able to tell me which company has the towing contract for the Long Island Railroad Tunnel. Yours, by any chance?"

"We wish," Jones said emphatically.

"I think it is the Moran's," Ericsson mused. The tug was pitching a bit in heavy swells as she entered the lower harbor. Ericsson steered toward the Brooklyn shore.

I had been afraid that it was Moran. It was the biggest tug outfit in New York and I'd have a hell of a time pinpointing the right boat.

"Didn't McAllister get that?" asked Jones. That was another big one.

"No," said Ericsson. He opened the voice pipe and called, "Hey, you down there. Who got the Long Island Railroad Tunnel contract?"

"Gulf Atlantic," the voice came back.

"What does he know down there?" growled Jones.

"I still think it was Moran."

"One way to find out," said Jones. He turned to the big radio next to the wheel and played with the dials until he'd raised another tug. He traded insults and asked the question.

"Moran."

"I thought so," said Ericsson.

"Thanks a lot," I said. "I really appreciate it."

"Should I find out which tug it was?" asked Jones.

"Would you? You'd save me a real hassle."

"Sure. Where was the barge picked up and what time?"

"Welfare Island, last night about midnight."

Jones proceeded to make a bunch of calls. I leaned against the dashboard and watched the Brooklyn waterfront glide by. Ericsson steered with one hand and sipped coffee with the other.

"What company are you with?" I asked.

"Sadie Brown Towing and Salvage Enterprises, Ltd., Inc."

"Oh."

"Never heard of it?"

"Can't say that I have."

Ericsson chuckled, finished his coffee and took out a pipe. "We're a small outfit," he said. "Me, and Travis, and Gink, down below, and Sadie."

"Sadie's the boat?"

"Right. We took her off the bottom of Gravesend Bay. She'd rammed a sub."

"In Gravesend Bay?"

"Some kind of secret new one. The Navy didn't want the papers to find out, so they paid off the owners and looked the other way when we raised her. Gink dropped in a diesel he found somewhere and we were in business."

Jones was still working the radio. *Sadie Brown* was nearing the Verrazano Bridge.

"How's business?"

Ericsson sighed. "Slow. People like the big companies. They don't think of us yet 'cause we haven't been around that long. Besides, any big job they need two or three tugs and all we have is one."

"There must be smaller jobs around."

"There are. But often they don't pay. They know we can't fight them."

"Sounds tough."

Ericsson brightened. "We make up for it with salvage." The boat rocked in the wake of a Staten Island ferry.

"What kind of salvage?" I asked. Ericsson seemed to want to talk.

"Pier reclamation, mostly." He jiggled the wheel and the rocking stopped.

I glanced across at him. He kept his eye on the water ahead. Jones rose from the radio with a satisfied sigh, and kneaded his back muscles.

"Deborah Moran," he said.

"You got it already?" I asked, excited.

"That's your boat. She picked up the barge around midnight and pushed it over to the Waterside project. Know where that is?"

I said, "I can't thank you enough. It's along the East River right below the U.N., right?"

"Yeah."

"Fantastic," I said.

"Let me ask you something, Creegan. The guys on *Deborah Moran* said the barge was full of mud. What's so special about the mud?"

"I lost something in it."

Jones and Ericsson exchanged looks. "How you going to find it in a whole bargeful of mud?" asked Jones.

"It will take awhile," I said.

"Won't people wonder what you are doing?" asked Ericsson. It was a good question. I tried to picture myself sliding around the barge with a metal detector. The idle and curious would gather. They might include the police.

"Yes," I said slowly. "That could be a problem. I'll have to wait until dark."

"What you going to see in the dark?" asked Jones.

"It might be difficult," I admitted.

"You have a problem," said Jones. "Mind me asking what the thing you're looking for is?"

"I'm terribly sorry, but I do."

"It is possible we can offer a solution," said Ericsson. "What would it be worth to you to move that barge to a more private location where you could search for whatever it is you want without fear of discovery?" He cast a crafty eye at me. Both men were alert to my reactions.

"It might be worth quite a lot to me," I said. "But I wouldn't have any funds until I found what I am looking for."

"But if someone moved that barge, you would pay when you could?"

"Certainly."

Jones and Ericsson looked at each other. I moved aside to let them talk. They muttered briefly, then Jones said, "You're on. We'll move the barge."

"I think I should tell you it's not my barge," I said.

"Barges often slip their moorings. When you're through looking, we'll bring it back and say we found it adrift."

"Why are you doing this?" I asked.

"You're going to pay handsomely," said Ericsson.

"How much?"

"Five thousand dollars."

I had never hired a tug to move a barge before, but it sounded steep. On the other hand, five thousand for a million bucks of coins wasn't bad. "I'd pay it," I said. "But it will take awhile."

"How long awhile?" asked Jones.

"After I find what I'm looking for, I have to sell it. And that will take some time."

Ericsson looked troubled. "I'm sorry, Creegan. I must ask this. Have you stolen something?"

"I have *taken* something."

"You mean you just took something lying around?" asked Jones.

"I'm not a thief," I said. I thought a moment and took a stab. "What I've done is sort of like, oh . . . like let's say a building has been abandoned and pretty soon it's going to fall down or burn up and you see something nice, like a fireplace mantle or something like that, so you go and take it off the wall and carry it out. Or maybe you go around to old piers and remove docking cleats that are just going to be lost when the pier collapses into the water. That sort of thing." I smiled.

Jones laughed. "All right."

Ericsson nodded. "We're performing a service. We remove only those that are unsafe."

"What do you do with them?" I asked.

"We sell the iron ones to marinas and yacht clubs as decorations. Now and then we find a brass cleat. They're worth a fortune melted down. Gink does it. He's got a little smelter."

"It gets us by day to day," said Jones. "Enough to keep Sadie, anyhow."

"So do we have a deal?" I asked.

"Hang on," said Ericsson. He spun the wheel and *Sadie Brown* heeled sharply into a tight 180-degree turn. Ericsson aimed the bow at the tip of Manhattan and uncapped the voice pipe. "Ahead full," he ordered crisply.

The pipe spewed Gink's indignant howl. "Turn like that once more without warning me and I'll cut your rudder linkage."

"Ahead full," bellowed Ericsson. "And keep your below-decks backtalk to yourself."

"Where we going?" asked Gink.

"Towing job. Ahead full."

"Aye aye, sir."

Sadie Brown trembled with the increased thrust, buried her stern and cleaved a fat, white bow wake up the bay toward Manhattan.

Chapter 14

Ericsson looked worried as we neared the barge at the edge of Waterside. Landfill had created a broad expanse that ran for ten city blocks. Several large buildings were already under construction between the water's edge and the F.D.R. Drive.

"She's sitting mighty high," said Jones.

"I noticed," replied Ericsson. "Snub up the bow and we'll have a look." Jones scrambled down the wheel house ladder and waited in the bow, a neatly coiled rope in his right hand.

"What's wrong?" I asked.

"We'll see in a minute," Ericsson muttered.

"Do you want me to take the stern line?"

"We can handle her." The stretch of water between the barge and the tug narrowed. Ericsson had already ordered half-speed. Now he called for reverse.

Neatly, like a lady pausing to chat across a picket fence, *Sadie Brown* came alongside the barge. Jones flipped his line over a post and snubbed it tight to the tug. Ericsson called for ahead slow and spun the wheel to the left. With the bow line tight and the rudder all the way over, the slowly turning screw held the tug immobile.

Ericsson tied the wheel and stepped onto the catwalk that circled the wheel house. He turned with an unhappy look and motioned me outside. I joined him and saw the problem. The barge was empty.

"They've already off-loaded," said Ericsson.

"Godammittohell."

"There's the mud," said Ericsson, pointing at a heap of mud next to a small steam shovel. "Sorry."

I was a lot sorrier. Ericsson's idea of spiriting the barge away to a quiet spot where I could search it at my leisure had lifted my spirits considerably.

The coins were probably scattered under the mudpile like fish eggs in the ocean. Even if the steam shovel had scooped most of them in one bite, they'd probably be at the bottom of the pile, as they'd been on the top of the barge.

Jones called up to us. "Empty?"

"Yup," said Ericsson.

"Thought so. She was riding too high. Now what?"

He and Ericsson looked at me. "I don't know," I said.

Ericsson looked as disappointed as I felt. But all he'd lost was a towing job. I brightened a little. In some ways it had been a successful venture. At least I'd found the mud, and presumably the coins. That had to be part of the battle. I'd have to work out a way to search the mudpile. As I stared at it, I became almost elated. The landfilled piles were nearly deserted. The only people in sight were workmen on a half-completed high-rise apartment building. Trucks rumbled in and out of the area but didn't come very near the water's edge. With luck, and a good metal detector, there was no reason why I couldn't find at least some of the coins. It would take time, but with Rifkins, Burke and Kosinski helping, we could sift through the bargeload of mud in a few days and nights, provided no one moved it. And that wasn't likely, because it had apparently reached its final resting place.

"I'm sorry this hasn't worked out," I said to Ericsson. Jones, who had joined us on the catwalk, shrugged.

"What's in that pile of mud?"

"Something I lost."

"I mean what was it?"

"I can't go into that. I'm not in this alone and it wouldn't be right to tell."

"Do you want to get off here?" said Ericsson.

"Yes. And thank you very much for all your trouble." I wanted to give them something, but I only had about ten bucks in my pocket in addition to the two gold coins. And though I considered giving them one of the coins, I couldn't risk tipping them off. There was nothing to stop them from coming back for a closer look.

"I wish I could pay you somehow, but at the moment . . ."

"Don't worry about it."

"I feel I should. If anything comes of this, I'll send you something, how's that?"

"If you like," said Ericsson. His cloudy blue eyes were unreadable.

Jones leaned over the side and yelled into the open engine-room door, "Hey, Gink."

Gink stuck out an oil-splattered dirty face. "What now?"

"You got any of those cards?"

He reached into the bib pocket of his overalls and handed up a smudged business card, which Jones relayed to me.

It said, "Sadie Brown Towing and Salvage Enterprises, Ltd., Inc.," and had a phone number in the lower left-hand corner.

"Thanks," I said. "I'll get in touch."

"You do that. Who knows? Maybe you'll need a towing job after all."

Jones untied the bow and Ericsson nosed *Sadie Brown* along the pier until I found a place to jump down. I waved, but the tug was already heading back out into the mainstream.

Feeling vaguely rotten, I strolled over to the mudpile. It was about twenty feet high and forty feet in diameter. White ice crystals glinted where the bitter cold had crusted the surface. I gave it a tentative poke and someone yelled, "Hey, you."

A middle-aged guy who looked like a retired cop was walking briskly toward me. He wore a private guard uniform.

"What are you doing?" he asked sternly.

"Just taking a walk," I said mildly.

"Well, walk on out of here. This is private property."

"Sorry. I wasn't doing anything."

"The gate's that way," said the guard. He pointed with a short nightstick. I shrugged and walked away, feeling his eyes on me until I reached the street.

Night was coming in rapidly, and with the sun gone the cold became bitter. I walked a few blocks, aimlessly, until the thought of a nice hot dinner with Jeannie and a night, perhaps, in her warm bed drove me into a telephone booth.

She answered on the first ring.

"Hi," I said.

"Hello. How'd it go?"

"I found the mud."

"Beautiful. What about the other stuff?"

"Is someone there?"

After a moment's silence, she said, "As a matter of fact, yes."

"Loren?"

"None of your business," Jeannie said cheerfully. "Where'd you find the mud?"

I tried to sound casual. "I'll tell you if you tell me."

"I don't know about that," she mused.

The cold and the long day conspired to make me short-tempered. "Dammit, Jeannie, who the hell is there?"

"Easy, Hog."

"Don't easy me, I love you."

"Hang on." I heard her say away from the phone, "Loren, will you check the roast? In the kitchen." She came back on the phone. "Still there?"

"Yes."

"All right. Loren is here. I like you very much, too much, probably. You don't know if you love me, which is the way I feel about you, but don't crowd me, Hog. I've been on my own for a long time and I like it that way."

"Sorry."

"And don't apologize."

"I found the mud at Waterside."

"What about the coins?"

"Presumably in the mud. I'll go back tomorrow if I can figure a way."

"Great. I can't help you in the morning, I have a call, but I'll come over in the afternoon."

"Wonderful, enjoy your dinner."

"Thank you, Hog. Take care of yourself."

"Sure." I said goodby, hung up, and stared at the menu in the luncheonette where I had found the phone. After some deep thought, I ordered the house-special hamburger. Then I took a subway uptown and a cab over to Welfare Island to see how the strike was going and to try to get hold of Rifkins and Burke and Kosinski.

Chapter 15

The hoghouse was jammed with half the membership of Local 147. I located Burke in the area with the loudest yelling. Kosinski was with him. Rifkins leaned against the far wall with a couple of other foremen, none of whom looked happy. Burke was engaged in a shouting match with a shop steward across the room. Old Kavanaugh sat next to the man on a pile of beds shoved against the wall. He grinned as Burke tore into the other shop steward, accusing the union official of selling out. When Burke finished, Kavanaugh nodded approval.

"You've a decent set of lungs, Burke."

"Goddamn right," yelled Burke. The shop steward he was assaulting looked uncomfortable. Burke noticed I was standing next to him.

"Find it?" he whispered. Ten men cocked their ears our way.

"Quiet," I muttered. "Yes, I found it."

"Where?"

"Waterside."

"Great."

"We're going to have a hell of a time getting it."

"Why?"

I explained about the site and the guard. Kosinski leaned toward us and listened gravely. After I finished describing the mudpile and suggested that we had to get a metal detector, I asked how the strike was going.

"Fantastic," said Burke. "We shut down the water tunnels, the sewage tunnel and the crosstown subway."

I looked at him. The four of us had put a couple of thousand people out of work.

"They say the Teamsters are coming over," Burke added.

A sudden cheer shook the rafters. I looked up. Kavanaugh was struggling to his feet. He cleared his throat and spoke, the demonic fire bright in his eyes.

"Shelter ... food ... dignity.... That is all the working man has ever asked." He glanced around the room of men young enough to be his grandchildren. "A simple request," he continued in a lilting, sing-song voice. "A fair request ... a righteous request." Again he paused and scanned the room as if hunting out company spies. "But requests unanswered become *demands*. And now we *demand* our shelter. We *demand* our food. We *demand*, above all, our dignity. *And we shall have it.*"

A ragged cheer exploded into a crescendo of applause as Kavanaugh raised his arms over his head. An iron man behind me remarked to another, "I don't know about this food and shelter crap, but Kavanaugh knows his ass about dignity."

"Go to your homes," said Kavanaugh. "Report when

you should for picket duty, and keep posted. Things will move quickly now." He glanced at a piece of paper. "Would Brother Burke, Brother Kosinski and Brother Creegan see me before they leave?"

"What the hell?" said Burke.

The room emptied quickly. I walked over to Kavanaugh. Burke and Kosinski followed.

Kavanaugh nodded briskly. "The muckety-mucks want to see you over at the office."

"The who?" I asked.

"The muckety-mucks," Kavanaugh muttered. "Don't let them push you around, boys."

We discovered, at the office, that the muckety-mucks were our own union's higher-ups, gabardine-suited men of the generation between Kavanaugh's and mine. They smoked cigars and looked slick and the way they treated us made me understand why Kavanaugh called them muckety-mucks.

"Close the door," said one of them. Burke kicked it shut.

The other said, with a broad smile, "Hello, boys." He was Carson, president of the local, and the guy I'd voted against. "Looks like we've started a little trouble."

I said nothing.

Carson frowned. "The way I hear it, Reese caught you guys stealing something and that old coot Kavanaugh turned it into a revolution."

Carson was talking big, but every man in the room knew that even in semi-retirement, Kavanaugh did what he damned well pleased.

"Not exactly," I said.

Carson turned marble eyes on me. "What did happen? Who are you . . . Creegan?"

"Creegan."

"What happened, Creegan?"

"Reese and a guy from the museum thought we'd taken artifacts out of the heading. They told us we had to empty our pockets."

"Did you?"

"Did we what?"

"Take artifacts." He scratched his shiny head. "Artifacts, Creegan?"

"That's what the museum guy said."

"Did you take them?"

"Of course not."

"So why didn't you empty your pockets?"

"Why the hell should we?" snarled Burke. He was growing restive in the small room. I noticed it was Reese's office, which probably meant that the union and the company were talking privately. It wouldn't do them much good, however, until they got the men on their side, and for the moment it seemed that everyone was having too much fun listening to Kavanaugh. Wildcat strikes are a nice break in the routine. From the worried looks on the faces of Carson and his henchman, I surmised that they feared the wildcat was about to get out of hand.

Carson smiled blandly. "We're not at war with the company, you know. The general idea is that they want to build a tunnel and we help them. But you guys . . . and Kavanaugh . . . what do you want?"

"Food, shelter and dignity," said Burke with a straight face.

Carson grimaced. "Look. If I get that yo-yo Reese to apologize to you guys, will that make you happy enough to talk Kavanaugh out of this nonsense?"

I shrugged. The strike freed us to dig out our coins. I

personally didn't care, because I'd pretty much decided never to go back into the tunnel regardless of whether we got the coins.

"Well, come on," snapped Carson. "This nonsense has gone on long enough."

Burke said, "The museum guy has to apologize too."

Carson assumed a puzzled expression. "This is something I don't quite follow. Who's this museum guy?"

"Ask the company," I said. "He was getting permission from the lawyers to go into the heading."

"The company says the lawyers never heard of him."

"He said he talked to them," said Burke.

Carson shook his head. "The on-site guys say that he walked in and *said* the company said it was O.K. or something like that. Nobody is sure what happened. They called the museum to see if he worked there and they said he does."

"So why'd he lie about the lawyers?" I asked.

"Sounds to me like he figured it was easier just to walk in than hassle with them," Carson replied.

I said, "I suppose so," but it puzzled me a little.

"Well, he started this," said Burke. "And he's got to apologize along with Reese."

"I'll see what I can do," Carson said doubtfully. "In the meantime could you do me a personal favor and talk Kavanaugh into being reasonable?"

"I don't understand," said Kosinski. He'd been silent since we'd entered the office, and Carson looked up in surprise and asked him who he was. Kosinski told him and added that he thought it was strange that the president of our local had to ask the rank and file to intercede with a shop steward. Carson mumbled something about Kavanaugh's popularity with the men. We agreed to talk to him and left.

We reported to Kavanaugh what Carson had said. He grinned maliciously and repeated his promise of a long strike. Then we found Rifkins and went over to Charley's to discuss how to find our coins.

Over a few drinks, we agreed that Rifkins and I would take one coin from each man to sell so we could buy a metal detector and rent a truck. We moved to a booth in the back so we wouldn't draw a crowd, took out our lumps and began scraping away the mud. I thought it was a good omen that all four lumps revealed gold coins, and ordered a round to celebrate.

Rifkins scooped them up and dropped them in his pocket. I toyed with my second lump, but we got back into a discussion of how we would search the muck, so I put it away.

We decided that the best way around the guards would be to approach the site as part of the work crew, which wouldn't be too hard as we were working men anyway. The details we decided to wing, and as the night wore on and the drinking continued, the idea sounded better and better.

Chapter 16

Rifkins was waiting outside Harry Holtzman's when I got there early the next morning. I introduced him to Harry, who scanned the coins with his glass.

"One of these is a beauty," he said.

"What's it worth?"

"Perhaps two thousand dollars."

"Sold," said Rifkins.

"I can't buy it. I can take it on consignment, though. I shouldn't have too much trouble disposing of it."

"We need cash," I said.

"I haven't got that kind of money."

"What about the others?"

"Five hundred apiece."

"Sold," said Rifkins.

Holtzman played with a tea bag. "Please understand. I don't usually deal in such large numbers. I have a small business."

"How long is consignment?" I asked.

"I can't guarantee that. A week. Perhaps a month."

"Too long."

"How much money do you need?" he asked.

Rifkins and I looked at each other. I decided to play it straight with Harry. "We need enough to buy a good metal detector."

The coin dealer smiled knowingly. "They don't run much more than a hundred dollars."

"We need the best."

"Tell you what. Leave me the coins. I'll give you a hundred dollars down on each and otherwise treat it as a consignment sale."

Rifkins looked doubtful. Harry noticed and asked if we would watch the shop while he bought a pack of cigarettes.

"Do you trust this guy?" Rifkins asked as soon as he had left.

"I'm pretty sure about him. But it doesn't really matter. We need a few hundred bucks. He'll give it to us. Even if he doesn't give us anything else, and I doubt that would happen, we'll get our metal detector, find the rest of the coins and be rich. What do we care about a few thousand bucks?"

"If we find the other coins."

"We will."

When Harry came back we told him we would accept his offer. He gave us a check on a bank around the corner that cashed it willingly. Then we found a sporting-goods store that had a metal detector for a hundred and fifty bucks and we were in business. It consisted of a long metal pole with a dish-like protuberance at the bottom and a read-out dial on the handle. It was powered by batteries and fit in a belt carrier. Rifkins tried to put the thing on in the cab to the truck rental place, but the belt would not encircle his girth.

Having used their vehicles once to help a friend move, I chose the Slapner Truck Rental Agency, because they supplied battered old trucks that looked like the kind struggling independent contractors would rent. We were given a hideous orange step van that seemed to be leaning against the garage wall. It was covered with mud, two windows were broken and the rear doors wouldn't close. The brake felt like foam rubber and the clutch seemed rusted in place. The Slapner attendant gassed it up and warned, "Don't get it dirty or play the radio."

I told him I wouldn't, stomped the clutch down with both feet, found some kind of forward gear and lurched into traffic. Rifkins, perched on an orange crate next to me, clasped the door handle. When we reached the building site, Burke and Kosinski hopped in. Burke saw the metal detector and grabbed.

"Lemme have it."

Rifkins let Burke carry it after Kosinski wrapped his coat around it. We headed for the river, leaving the truck out on the street until we got a clear picture of what we were going to do.

"It's right around here," I said as we passed the last building. Then I stared at the flat ground between us and the river. Burke knew instantly.

"Oh no," he wailed.

Rifkins growled a curse.

The pile was gone.

Chapter 17

We'd lost it again.

Kosinski said, "They spread it out."

"Christ on a crutch," said Burke.

I thought the same thing.

The large dip between the two buildings nearest the river was now filled with the mud from our tunnel. A bulldozer was leveling the last bumpy spots. Apparently they were using our mud to build a parking lot. And our bags of gold coins were probably scattered over the entire half-acre site. We'd never find them all.

We found a sheltered spot in one of the half-completed buildings and sat down to wait for the bulldozer to go away. It was cold and damp. An hour passed.

"Will you stop futzing around," Burke snarled at the distant bulldozer operator. "It's smooth enough."

Apparently the operator didn't think so. After he had

spread the mud evenly, he proceeded to back his machine the length of the field, over and over again, dragging his lowered blade behind him like an ant returning home with a morsel for his community.

"Hey, kid," said Burke. "Get some coffee."

He was talking to me. I stopped answering to "kid" when I turned nineteen, so I ignored him.

"Creegan," said Rifkins. "Why don't you get some coffee?"

I took up a collection and went in search of a coffee shop. It was better than huddling in the cold. When I got back, the bulldozer was being jockeyed onto a flat-bed trailer. The four of us drank coffee. With luck we would be able to start our search in a few minutes.

The trailer rig pulled the bulldozer away. Aside from some men working on the upper floors of one of the buildings, we were alone. Burke slipped the metal detector's belt around his huge waist. Then I smelled something. It was a thick heavy odor like burning rubber.

"Hold it," Kosinski said. "Something's coming."

With a throb of engines and a smell of hell, three immense black trucks lumbered around the corner and onto the parking field. Signs on the trucks said, "Big Apple Asphalt." A moment later another flat-bed trailer swung into the area, carrying a steamroller.

"I don't believe this," said Burke.

I didn't either. We crept back into our shelter, as the men from Big Apple Asphalt proceeded to dump steaming mounds of blacktop all over the parking field. As each truck emptied, it roared off around the buildings and disappeared.

The steamroller rolled ponderously off its flat-bed and waited on the sidelines. Then a tremendous square vehicle snorted up and began spreading the black piles. It was a grader, and as it graded the steamroller moved along behind it, flattening the surface into a rock-hard shell.

"Screw this," said Rifkins. "We'll never get them now."

"The metal detector can still locate them," I said. "All we have to do is dig through the blacktop."

"That's all?"

He had a point. The asphalt looked to be about six inches deep and the cold was hastening its hardening.

"We need a jackhammer."

Rifkins looked weary. "And where do we get a jackhammer?"

"Rent one," said Kosinski.

"And then just jackhammer up this brand-new parking lot?" said Rifkins. He had another point. Someone might ask us what we were up to. I thought a moment.

"Steal one."

"What good will that do?"

"Steal one from Con Ed."

"Yeah," said Burke. "I see what you mean."

"I don't," said Rifkins.

"We'll steal a Con Ed truck. Then we'll set up barricades and signs and we'll look like we're doing what we're supposed to be doing." It was a neat little plan. Con Ed is short for Consolidated Edison, which is the outfit that supplies electricity and gas in New York City and digs up the streets. There is no more common sight in the city than a blue and white Con Ed truck parked next to a hole in the road with a guy bouncing around on a jackhammer.

"If no one stops us from digging up their parking lot, someone will see we have the stolen truck," Rifkins worried aloud.

"Who?" I said. "There's ten thousand Con Ed trucks. Ours will look just the same. Besides, the guys whose truck it is will probably go out for a few beers before they report it stolen."

"I don't know," said Rifkins.

"It'll work," said Burke. "Come on. They're almost done with the asphalt." They were by now. The trucks were gone and the grader and steamroller were finishing up a final corner.

Burke was already walking off toward First Avenue, presumably in search of a truck to steal. Rifkins looked pleadingly at Kosinski and me.

"I'll stay and keep an eye on things," I said. "You and Kosinski go with Burke."

Rifkins and Kosinski shook their heads.

"We're in this together," said Kosinski. "We'll all go. This parking lot isn't going anywhere."

We caught up with Burke, who was carrying the metal detector like a walking stick. He grinned belligerently.

By chance Con Ed had a big generating plant a few blocks up First Avenue. There was sure to be an abundance of trucks. But when we got there it proved impossible to get in to grab a truck and get it out because there was a guard at the gate. So we hailed a cab and had the driver cruise up First and then down Second until we found a Con Ed crew at work.

They had closed off two lanes of traffic. A barricade draped with yellow vinyl surrounded an open manhole. An air pump ran noisily and two men leaned on the barricade chatting and handing tools down into the manhole. We got out of the cab and watched from the doorway of a hardware store.

The truck had a small compressor and a jackhammer. It was just what we needed. The problem was the two guys standing around the hole. We waited a few minutes, hoping they would disappear for coffee or a snooze, but they didn't.

The hardware store owner came out to see what the four of us were doing blocking his entrance. We moved down to a meat market. But when its customers began to stare as they walked in and out, Rifkins said, "Spread out."

He pointed at a tobacconist's. "You and Burke go there," he said to me. "Me and Kosinski'll be by the laundry."

Burke and I shuffled off to the tobacconist's and pretended we were pipe smokers. Rifkins and Kosinski leaned against the laundry window like a pair of wrecking cranes at rest.

Suddenly one of the Con Ed workers dropped into the manhole. The other crouched down, looking in.

Burke lunged forward. "Now's our chance."

"What are you going to do?" I asked, darting alongside.

"Clip the son of a bitch behind the ear and drop him in the hole," muttered Burke, stealing through the pedestrians on the sidewalk like a stalking rhinoceros.

"You can't just slug the guy," I protested.

"Watch me."

I looked back, but Rifkins and Kosinski were already edging toward the truck. Burke drew back his fist, but the Con Ed worker must have sensed us behind him because he suddenly whirled around, an uncertain look on his face.

Burke's face must have cleared up any uncertainty for him because he raised his arms protectively and tried to maneuver into a more defensible position. Unfortunately for him, the only defensible position against somebody the size and temper of Burke was across the street—and he wasn't.

"What . . . ?" the guy asked.

"In the hole," snarled Burke.

"What?"

"Feet first or head first?" asked Burke. "All the same to me."

"What, are you crazy?" The guy was small and dark and wiry and talked like he came from Queens. Woodside, perhaps, and such guys aren't easily pushed around. He was recovering from his surprise—his eyes darted around as if he were hunting for something to bend over Burke's head. There was going to be bloodshed and commotion.

I pulled out my wallet and extracted a fifty, change from our metal detector, and held it in front of the guy. Then I said, "Look. We want you in that hole. I'd appreciate it if you would take this as an expression of my personal gratitude for going quietly." The guy looked at the fifty and hesitated.

"Save your money," snapped Burke. "He's going in the hole."

"Oh yeah?" said the guy. As I said, he was from Woodside.

"Yeah," said Burke.

"Take the money," I pleaded.

"Why do you want me in the hole?" asked the guy. Burke grabbed him by the jacket. The guy pawed at his belt and came up with a heavy pair of pliers. I rammed my shoulder between them, shoved the fifty into the guy's shirt pocket and said, "Get in the hole."

"You're going to steal the truck," the guy said.

"Right."

"What will I tell the other guys?"

"If you're an idiot you'll tell them I gave you a fifty to get out of our way. But if you're not an idiot maybe you'll think of something."

He slipped his pliers back in his pocket, and jumped into the hole. Burke and I grabbed the inner manhole cover with the steel hooks lying next to it and dragged it over the hole. It weighed about two hundred pounds. Then we dropped the outer cover on top of it and picked up the barricades and the traffic signs and threw them in the back of the truck.

Kosinski was at the wheel, Rifkins next to him. Burke and I jumped in the back and Kosinski floored it.

Chapter 18

There was a traffic jam along the road that led to the interior of the Waterside project. It consisted of fourteen black limousines heading in.

"Now what?" Burke growled.

Kosinski drove to the end of the line of long black cars. The line moved jerkily forward. Several minutes later we reached the now completed parking field and parked a ways down from the cluster of cars already there.

"What is going on?" Burke asked. The rest of us didn't know.

In the time it had taken us to steal a Con Ed truck, someone had painted yellow lines on the blacktop, and someone else had erected a small grandstand along the side. A third someone was running wires from a sound truck to a podium in front of the stands. He said "testing" several times and "testing" crackled around the walls of the half-built apartment complex.

In the meantime more cars, mostly black and official-looking, continued to enter the lot. Their occupants stayed inside, probably because it was cold. Only a few brave souls braved the little grandstand's exposed seats.

"Am I nuts," asked Burke, "or is somebody getting ready to make a speech?"

Kosinski was staring out the windshield, his chin resting on the steering wheel. He cleared his throat, started to speak, seemed to reconsider, and said nothing.

Rifkins nervously played his fingers over his nose. He fidgeted with his feet and an occasional tic wracked the left side of his face. His eyes flicked like metronomes from the podium to a police car next to the stands. He nudged Kosinski. "Let's get out of here," he muttered.

"No," said Kosinski.

"The cops will spot us," said Rifkins.

"No they won't."

"Am I nuts," asked Burke, "or is somebody getting ready to make a speech?"

I answered slowly. "There's a podium and a microphone and a grandstand and a lot of people obviously waiting for an event to begin. Therefore, you are probably not nuts and I agree that it looks like somebody is getting ready to make a speech."

"Why?"

"Now that is less obvious," I said. I felt like I was in the midst of explaining a dream to myself while still asleep. "Because there doesn't really seem to be a reason for a speech. Here we are on a new parking lot in the middle of four half-built apartment buildings on the shore of the East River on a cold winter day."

"Maybe it's a political rally," said Burke.

"I doubt that," I answered, "unless whoever is running for what is counting heavily on the seagull and sailor vote, which, as far as I know, has never been that important in city politics."

"Let's get out of here," said Rifkins. No one replied. Suddenly sirens wailed and two motorcycle cops roared in, followed by a flag-draped limousine. People leaped out of the parked cars and hurried to the grandstand. The police escort pulled up in front of the podium and a moment later a youngish, athletic-looking guy hopped out of the back and climbed the two wooden steps to the microphone. An older man joined him. Scattered applause drifted from the stands. A four-man–one-woman camera and sound crew began recording the event.

The older man tapped the microphone. Little electronic clicks indicated it was live. He spoke rapidly about progress and housing and the exploits of the present mayor's administration. He made several light remarks about the man he was about to introduce that received laughter from the audience.

"It's a dedication ceremony," I said disbelievingly.

"Dedicating what?" asked Burke.

"Listen." The older man rambled on, building up his introduction. Burke looked at me. "Do you hear what I hear?"

I nodded.

"Do you guys follow him?" Burke asked Kosinski and Rifkins.

"I don't believe it," said Rifkins.

"He's dedicating the parking lot," said Kosinski.

Burke breathed a sigh of relief. "I thought it was just me," he said. "It's them. They're crazy."

"Here's more of them," I said. Several more cars raced

in, also escorted by wailing police. Out stepped a half-dozen more city officials, several of whom I recognized from newspaper photographs. "This is going to take awhile," said Kosinski.

Then something happened that made waiting impossible. The second man, having been introduced, was well into a speech about middle-class tax bases when a truck marked De Jay Fencing rumbled in and disgorged a crew of laborers and several dozen rolls of cyclone fence. Ignoring the speechmakers, they began digging holes and dropping in fence posts and cement.

Burke started jumping around the cab of the truck. "They're closing it up," he yelled. "We'll be locked out."

It looked like he was right.

The four of us huddled and came up with a plan. Kosinski, Burke and Rifkins drove away, leaving me in the grandstand to keep an eye on things and signal them if there was trouble.

Half an hour passed, with speech after speech lauding the middle-class parking lot in the middle of all the middle-class housing. The fence crew was working quickly. Already one side of the lot was blocked off. I got nervous and watched the entrance for the Con Ed truck. Ten more minutes passed. Then Jeannie's Rollswagen appeared, hesitantly. After circling the area slowly, she parked at the far end and emerged tall and leggy with Howard at her side.

I stood up and waved frantically while she looked around. When she spotted me she waved back and hurried toward the stand. In the time it took her to cross the parking lot and climb up to where I was, the speaker lost his audience. Every eye in the stands followed Jeannie and Howard as if they and only they had the answer to the housing problem in Manhattan.

"Hi, Hog," she said gaily. "What's happening?"

I kissed her and said, "They were dedicating the parking lot until you got here. Now they're considering giving it to you."

"How nice. But I already have garage space."

"The lot is worth more."

"How come?"

"It's paved with gold."

"Our gold?"

"Landfill. Under the blacktop." I explained how that had come to be.

"What are you going to do about it?" Jeannie asked.

"We're already doing it," I said. "See?"

She looked where I pointed. Burke and Kosinski and Rifkins were back. "What?"

"That Con Ed truck. Burke and the others are in it."

"What's that long thing sticking out the front?"

"A metal detector." According to plan, they had welded the metal detector to the chassis so that it protruded out like a frog's tongue, inspecting what lay beneath the surface directly in front of the truck. They had the beeper device inside the cab. In theory, they could circle the parking lot without looking suspicious while they located our gold.

Speeches were still going strong. The housing administrator was at it now, explaining to his audience of other city officials how Waterside would offer housing to poor as well as middle-class people. As he droned on, the Con Ed truck commenced a circular sweep of the parking lot. It was moving at about five miles per hour and tracking back and forth in plain sight of fifty or so people and ten cops. I kept a close eye on the cops.

Suddenly the blue and white truck went into a circle that spiraled tighter and tighter. Its brake lights flashed and it stopped abruptly, nosing forward on the front springs. The housing administrator introduced the mayor's deputy assistant counsel.

A moment later Burke, Kosinski and Rifkins hopped out of the cab and commenced setting up a barrier festooned with men-working signs. Then Rifkins set out a circle of red stanchions, which he connected with a blue plastic streamer.

Burke started the compressor. It was one of the new, quieter models, and interfered only slightly with the sound truck. The mayor's deputy assistant counsel raised his voice and continued smoothly.

Then Kosinski hauled a jackhammer from the back of the truck and walked with it under one arm to a spot Burke was marking with white chalk. Burke stepped back with a flourish. Kosinski placed the bit of the jackhammer on the chalk mark, wiped his hands on his overalls, gripped the handles of the jackhammer, leaned his weight into it and hit the triggers.

RAT RAT RAT RAT TAT thundered off the surrounding buildings and flew at the grandstand like a horde of concrete bats. The audience covered their ears. I could tell the mayor's deputy assistant counsel was shouting because his mouth was open very wide, but there was no way to hear him. He turned away from the mike and yelled something to the man next to him. Of course I couldn't hear the beginning of his sentence, but when Kosinski stopped the jackhammer, everyone heard rather clearly the end, ". . . SHOVE THAT THING UP HIS ASS . . ."

Several reporters scribbled in their notebooks. The mayor's deputy assistant counsel blanched and resumed speaking to his original subject in normal tones. Kosinski looked up in my direction. I made hand motions to indicate that he should drill quietly. As we were separated by about three hundred feet he misinterpreted "quietly" as "all clear."

RAT RAT RAT TRAT RAT TAT.

Again the audience covered their ears and again the mayor's deputy assistant counsel screamed into the mike futilely. He stepped back and yelled at the man next to him, who hurried over to a cop and pointed at Kosinski. I stood up and waved at Burke and pointed toward the cop, who was already walking toward the Con Ed truck. Burke leaped into the back of the truck. He reappeared immediately and set up a sign that said "Emergency."

When the cop saw the sign he returned to the foot of the podium and spoke with the city official. Kosinski kept drilling. By now every eye, including those of the speaker, was fastened on the Con Ed truck. Kosinski kept at it without pause. RAT RAT RAT RAT TRAT TRAT TAT RAT.

The mayor's deputy assistant counsel put his hands on his hips and waited. Rifkins stood by the widening hole in the asphalt with a pick in hand. Burke stood on the other side with a shovel. Kosinski kept drilling, turning up large chunks of frozen hard asphalt with expert twists of the pounding drill head.

The mayor's deputy assistant counsel jumped down angrily from the podium and began arguing with the cop. From where I sat, it looked like the cop was thoroughly enjoying defending the position that a Con Ed emergency took precedence over the speechmaking of a bunch of overpaid city officials. The arguing went on for several more minutes of arm waving and nose-to-nose shouting.

Finally the mayor's deputy assistant counsel pointed stiffly toward the Con Ed truck and the cop gave in. Fists balled, he strode toward the thundering jackhammer. I waved again and made throat-cut signs. Burke picked it up and tapped Kosinski on the shoulder. Kosinski nodded, extracted several more large chunks of blacktop and ceased drilling. By the time the cop reached them, Burke and Rifkins were digging by hand and Kosinski was replacing the jackhammer in the truck. The cop asked something and Kosinski nodded. Satisfied with the answer, the cop strolled back to the podium and apparently informed the mayor's deputy assistant counsel that the noise was over. He nodded curtly, climbed up to the mike and resumed his address.

Burke and Rifkins picked and shoveled with gusto. It looked like Kosinski had done all he had to. The hole was about six feet wide. They stacked chunks of asphalt around the edges. Rifkins broke up the underlying mud with his pick and Burke tossed it out. Suddenly he dropped the shovel and knelt down, pawing the dirt with his hands. Rifkins and Kosinski got very excited and jumped into the hole with him.

"They found something," Jeannie said.

"Beautiful." I wanted to run down there and dive into the hole to see for myself but it would have looked strange so I held back and waited impatiently for the speechmakers to go home.

Kosinski turned the truck around so that the back was right by the hole. Then, as Burke and Rifkins dug with their hands and placed things on the surrounding blacktop, Kosinski tossed them into the truck.

Fifteen minutes later the mayor's deputy assistant

counsel concluded his talk. He and several officials piled into a limousine that left with its police escort. The men and women in the stands clambered down hastily, scrambled into their waiting cars and drove off. Within five minutes we had the area to ourselves.

Jeannie and I rose, stiff with cold, climbed down the grandstand and headed for the Con Ed truck. Burke was ecstatic. "We found it. The whole load. Right here in one spot."

"Most of it," said Kosinski. "We were real lucky. The bags held a lot of it together."

"How many pieces?" I asked.

"Seven hundred and eight," he answered. About half.

"Here's more," said Rifkins. "I just found a whole 'nother bunch." He removed a ripped and sodden canvas bag and began tossing out more coins. I climbed in too to give him a hand. They had discovered the coins about two feet down.

The three of us worked in the hole for thirty or forty minutes, clawing through the mud and handing coin lumps up to Kosinski and Jeannie, who knocked off excess mud and dumped them in the truck. Howard sniffed curiously over the edge, making Burke nervous. Then after going five minutes without finding any more coins, I straightened up and asked Kosinski how many coins we had.

"Eleven hundred and four."

"I think that's about it in here," I replied. "Why don't you turn the truck around and sweep the detector over this area?"

He agreed and walked toward the cab. Jeannie stepped over to me and placed her hand on my head, which was easy because I was about two feet shorter than her, standing in the hole. Burke and Rifkins sat down on the edge and kneaded their back muscles.

Howard growled and moved toward Jeannie. "What's the matter, baby?" she asked him.

He didn't have to answer because we all saw Kosinski walking toward us with his hands in the air and a deadly expression on his face. Behind him was a tall man with a black hood over his head and a gun in his hand.

Chapter 19

Eye slots were cut in the black hood. The cloth rippled when the man spoke.

"Get in the hole." He prodded Kosinski with the gun and gestured briskly with his free hand at Jeannie. She stood stock still. Kosinski took her arm slowly and firmly and guided her into the hole. He stepped down in and turned around. The gunman stood with his back to the truck, training his weapon on the five of us. I stared in amazement.

Calmly, he said, "Everyone lie down. Slow."

"Who the hell are you?" asked Burke.

"Face down," said the gunman. "Now."

Howard growled softly. The man's eyes flicked inside the black cloth.

"I think we'd better do as he says," I said.

Kosinski nodded and knelt in the dirt. Burke thrust his

head belligerently forward. "You won't get away with this," he snarled.

"Does that mean I should shoot you?" Clouds of breath puffed out from the bottom of the hood. Burke stepped back, cockiness draining from his face. Howard stirred, rising from his sitting position. The gunman noticed.

"Howard," Jeannie hissed. "Come here."

"Everybody lie down," the gunman repeated.

Then I saw Kosinski eyeing the shovel. I prayed he wouldn't make a move for it. The gun looked like a .45 automatic and there's no such thing as a minor wound from such a weapon.

I knelt and pulled Jeannie down next to me. She was concentrating on Howard and seemed almost unaware of the gun. Several times she called his name, but he didn't respond.

"I'm driving out of here," the hooded man said. "I can watch you from the side mirrors. Don't anybody make me shoot."

"Just take it easy," I said as calmly as I could. "We don't want anyone hurt."

Howard stepped toward the man. He stiffened and pressed against the back of the truck. Howard's hackles rose, slightly, and his little ears lay back.

"Howard," Jeannie called, panic in her voice.

"Get him away from me," the man said tightly. The gun wavered from us toward Howard. Kosinski inched closer to the shovel.

"Let me come out and get him," Jeannie said. She sounded terrified.

"Don't move," the gunman said sharply. He seemed afraid of losing control of the situation. Howard took another step toward him, extending his head as he moved.

"Please," said Jeannie. "Let me get him." The man's eyes flickered from Howard to her. Kosinski extended his hand toward the shovel. The gunman saw him and whirled in a half crouch, gun pointed at Kosinski's head. *"Don't!"*

Kosinski froze. But the sudden movement startled Howard. He skittered sideways and growled deeply. The gunman whirled toward him as if to fire.

"No," shrieked Jeannie, throwing herself over the side of the hole and on top of Howard. The gun exploded while I was halfway to Jeannie. I landed on her and waited for a second shot. She remained on top of Howard, restraining his attempts to stand. I held her and looked up into the gun barrel.

"Just hold that animal like that," the hooded man said. The gun shook slightly. "The rest of you stay put." He walked in a wide circle toward the front of the truck so he could see all of us. Suddenly he leaped into the cab, started the engine and tore away.

I stayed on top of Jeannie until the truck was around the buildings. Then I let my breath out and stood, shaking. Jeannie was sobbing gently and stroking a small singed spot of Howard's fur, the only damage he'd suffered. I felt like kicking him in the slats for nearly getting us all killed. The shot that missed him could have hit Jeannie or any one of us.

Burke and Kosinski and Rifkins all yelled at once. Apparently they got over the shock of nearly getting killed faster than I because what they were upset about was the loss of our gold coins.

Rifkins was astonished. "How did he know?"

"Who was he?" asked Kosinski.

"Where's he going?" asked Burke.

"He's gone," said Rifkins.

"I don't understand," said Kosinski. That about summed it up. I didn't understand either. Apparently the hooded man had watched us dig up the coins. But how did he know they were coins? How did he know the Con Ed truck wasn't there legitimately?

"He must have been watching us," I ventured.

"But why?" three grown men on the verge of tears asked.

"He found out about the coins?"

"Nobody knows about them," snarled Burke.

"Yes. Harry Holtzman does—the guy Rifkins and I got the money from."

"Let's get him," yelled Burke.

"Wait. There's another guy. Sean Garfield."

"Who's he?"

I explained about the Numismatist Extraordinaire.

"Let's get him too. It's one of those guys. Maybe they're in it together." Burke was hopping up and down with a red face.

"Reese," said Kosinski. "And that museum guy."

"Byron?" yelled Burke.

"Yeah," Kosinski said doubtfully. "They didn't see 'em, though."

"The tugboat crew," I said. "But they didn't see them either."

"Anybody else?" Burke snarled.

"The salesman in the sports shop?"

"I doubt that," said Kosinski.

I agreed that it sounded unlikely.

"Anybody else, blabbermouth?" asked Burke.

"Don't jump on me, Burke."

"*I* didn't go around telling half the world about our coins, Creegan."

"Neither did I," I shot back.

"Knock it off," said Kosinski. "What about it, Creegan? Does anybody else know about the coins?"

I thought a moment. "No," I answered. "Just the two coin dealers, and maybe Reese and Byron and the tugboat crew, but none of them knew about the coins for sure. Just the dealers knew that."

"No one else could have known? You're sure?"

"I'm sure."

"What about you?" Kosinski asked Jeannie. "Did you tell anyone?"

She looked up blankly and shook her head, not yet over her scare. Howard, of course, responding to his mistress's concern, had fallen asleep where he lay.

"Let's get them coin dealers," Burke yelled. "Come on." He broke and ran toward First Avenue. It seemed like a good idea and the rest of us followed. When we caught up to him he had already nailed a taxi and was holding the door open yelling for us to hurry. The driver made some remark about too many people but by then we were already inside and urging him on. "Fortyseventh and Sixth," I said. It was after four by now and getting dark. Traffic was heavy and it took twenty minutes to get across town, enough time to discuss how lucky we were that the gunman's single shot missed us all.

I tried to imagine how Harry Holtzman could have engineered the coin heist, but I couldn't. I knew it was a mistake to put too much trust into what was actually just one nice afternoon of conversation together, but I had come away liking the man. It had to be Sean Garfield who took our coins.

"Where is he?" asked Burke as I strode across Forty-seventh.

"Garfield's place is first. Right along here someplace. Holtzman is a little farther down."

"There he is," Burke yelled. He grabbed for a door that said, "Coin Dealer."

"No. That's neither of them."

"Where?"

"Right up here, across the street, I think."

"You think?"

I was puzzled. I couldn't see Garfield's store. Rifkins, Kosinski and Jeannie caught up with us. "He can't find it," said Burke.

"Why?" asked Rifkins.

"It's right along here someplace. I was just here two days ago." I scanned the store fronts. There was a coin shop which wasn't it, a stamp store, a massage parlor, a cheap camera store and a hi-fi shop. Farther down was a coffee shop, another stamp store, a jeweler, a luggage store and then Harry Holtzman's. "Where the devil . . . I must have missed it. Back toward Sixth."

The others made rude remarks. Except Jeannie. I ignored them and hurried toward Sixth. No Garfield Coin Store. I began to think it was the wrong block. But it couldn't be because Holtzman's shop was there and I *knew* the stores were on the same block. I went back where I thought it should be and looked again. The others trailed behind me. A coin shop which wasn't it. A stamp store, a massage parlor, a cheap camera store. . . . I hadn't seen a massage parlor two days ago. I looked back.

A white sign with red letters ran along the top of the dark-draped plate-glass window.

GIRLS GIRLS GIRLS GIRLS GIRLS

Under that a smaller yellow sign said "NAME IT —WE HAVE IT."

Beneath that, in script, it said, Edwardian Delights.

And beneath that were neat black and gold letters invisible at first sight: Sean Garfield—Numismatist Extraordinaire.

"He's gone," I said.

"Who?"

"Garfield. Looks like he sold out to a massage parlor."

"That place?" asked Burke.

"That's where he was."

They gathered around me and gazed forlornly across the street at GIRLS GIRLS GIRLS GIRLS GIRLS.

"Maybe they know where he went?" said Jeannie.

"I doubt it."

"Let's ask," said Burke. We crossed the street. A foppishly dressed black man was lounging in the doorway. When he eyed us he straightened up and went into a spiel.

"Something for everyone, gentlemen. Come on in. The girls are great. The price is right. The time is now."

"Do you run this place?" I asked.

His eyes narrowed.

"The reason I ask is," I said smoothly, "I'm trying to locate the man who had a store here before you came."

"Never met the dude. However, if you'd care to enter our establishment perhaps one of the girls inside might know. And if she doesn't, you're here already so you might as well have some fun."

"Good idea," said Burke. "What do you say we all go in and have a little look around?"

"What about me?" asked Jeannie, stepping from behind Rifkins and Kosinski and becoming visible for the first time to the barker.

"*Hello* there," said the barker. "If you gentlemen would excuse me a moment ... honey, we got steady work and a good cut. Name your hours. We'll arrange things *your* way."

Jeannie looked doubtful. Burke said, "Come on, let's go in."

"That's not why we're here," said Rifkins.

"You heard the man, the girls might know."

"Like hell they would."

"What do you say, honey?" the barker asked Jeannie. "You'll clear three or four hundred a week with the look you're carrying."

"What about my friend?" Jeannie asked, tugging Howard in front of her. The barker stared, but recovered quickly.

"We'd find something for him."

"I want to check this place out," said Burke.

"No," said Rifkins.

"Has he had much experience?" the barker asked, pointing at Howard.

"Nothing commercial."

"How about yourself?"

"The same."

"I think I'll go talk to Holtzman," I said. "We're not going to learn anything here."

"I'm going in," said Burke.

"Suit yourself. I'll be back in a few minutes." I reached over and took Jeannie's hand. "Write if you find work."

"I'll be right here."

The barker heard that and seemed to realize Jeannie was putting him on. As I walked toward Holtzman's I heard him say, "Step right up. Step right up. The price is right. The time is now."

Harry was just closing up. "Hello," I said. "Got a minute?"

"A quick one. I didn't sell any of your coins yet."

Watching his face, I said, "That's not why I'm here."

"Oh?"

"Where's Garfield?"

"He left."

"I saw the massage parlor. Where'd he go?"

"I don't know."

"Why did he sell out his business?"

"I'm not sure that he did. He might have moved."

"You must know if he did."

Harry looked annoyed. "I don't."

"Were you surprised he moved?"

"I didn't know about it beforehand, if that's what you mean."

"When was the last time you saw him?"

"Why all the questions, young man?"

"Someone stole something from me. I think it might have been him."

"That doesn't sound likely."

"You said he was a crook."

"There are crooks and crooks. Sean is not the kind of crook who steals."

"When did you see him last?"

"I told you, he wouldn't steal."

"Someone stole a large number of gold coins from me and my friends."

157

Harry's eyes widened. "You found more."

"Many more," I said quietly. "It had to be him. Only two people knew about the coins. He and you."

"Why not accuse me, then?"

"You're still here. He left hurriedly. Where is he?"

Harry rubbed his eyes. Then he sighed deeply. "I find it hard to believe."

"So do I."

"What good will knowing where he is do you? You can't go to the police. You stole them too. Technically."

"I am painfully aware of that. But he stole them with a gun. My friends and I want them back."

Harry sighed. "He came in here yesterday. He paid me some money he owed me for a year. Not much. I never expected to see it again. Then he left."

"Did he say where he was going?"

"No."

"You didn't ask?"

"I thought he was going to his shop. When I went out to lunch I saw this 'GIRLS GIRLS GIRLS' stuff. It was the first I knew he was gone."

Chapter 20

"I don't love you and I never loved you."

"You can't mean that."

"I mean it."

"Darling. Seventeen years? And you never once loved me?"

"Well, once."

"When? When?"

"Uh." I flipped the page but I couldn't find the line.

"Hog," said Jeannie. "You're not helping."

I tossed the script on the coffee table and went to Jeannie's bar to refill my glass. "Want another?"

"No. Come on, Hog, I've got to get this on tape tonight."

"I'm sorry," I said. "I can't concentrate."

She turned off the recorder, crossed the room and

enveloped me in her long arms. "What's the matter, baby?"

"What do you think?" I downed half a glass of Scotch and tried to get out of her arms. "I lost a fortune today. I've got to find it."

"You'll find it."

"How?"

"You'll think it out. *We'll* think it out. Garfield can't just vanish. We'll find him and get the coins. But now, please, tonight I simply *must* record this scene." She kissed me lightly and I stopped trying to escape. "Come on, baby, just let's finish it. It'll clear your mind. Tomorrow we'll get Garfield." She removed the drink from my hand and led me back to the script. "Take it from 'Well, once.'"

I took it from "Well, once," and continued reading her through the portion of Loren's play that he wanted recorded so he could find out what was wrong with the dialogue. I had a fairly good idea myself what was wrong, and dialogue was only part of it. But Jeannie insisted we run through it, and though I suspected she was using it as therapy to calm me down, I went along.

I had left Harry Holtzman's convinced he couldn't tell me any more than he had. Jeannie was waiting outside GIRLS GIRLS GIRLS. She informed me that Burke was inside and that Rifkins and Kosinski, thoroughly disgusted with everything that had happened, had repaired to a nearby White Rose bar.

We found them and I related what Holtzman had said. Rifkins and Kosinski didn't say a word. They were solemnly passing back and forth a quart of Carstairs Rye, which they didn't offer to share. I babbled on for a few minutes until Rifkins raised a reddened eye in my direction. He didn't say a word, but it was clear that he and Kosinski were not inclined to chat. I told them I'd see them around.

Jeannie and Howard and I returned the rented truck and went back to her place.

"I think they're mad at you," she'd said.

"They don't have a right to be," I snapped back. "If it wasn't for me, none of this would have happened."

"I think that's why," said Jeannie. She placed a hand over my mouth before I could reply, and asked me to take her out for dinner. I told her I was broke. In that case, she said, she would take me out, which she did, and then back to the apartment to read the scene from Loren's play, which he had tentatively titled *A Nassau County Tragedy*.

The scene climaxed with Hubert, the character I was playing, slapping his unloved wife. I didn't slap Jeannie, of course, but her line was, "No, no, don't hit me," which she read with enough feeling to bring Howard into the room with most of his teeth hanging out. I froze.

Jeannie threw herself on him and explained that everything was all right. He sauntered out, with a backward warning glance at me. I unfroze and reached for my glass.

"Me too," said Jeannie.

I obliged.

"You read well," she said.

"Thanks." It was a nice thing to say. I thought I read terribly. I'd helped her a couple of times with lines and always felt wooden and uncomfortable.

"No, I really mean it," she said. "You got into Hubert very nicely."

"I want my gold coins."

"Why?"

"Why?" I yelled back, completely unnerved by her unexpected attitude.

"Yes, why?"

"Because they're mine, that's why."

"They weren't really yours."

"I found them, dammit, and Burke and Rifkins and Kosinski helped me get them out and they're mine. Or at least my share is mine."

She looked infuriatingly doubtful.

"And furthermore, Jeannie, I don't make a living going around acting and reading commercials. I shovel mud in a hole in the ground and I don't get that much in return. I'd like to have some money. Those coins are money."

She said nothing, but watched me blandly.

"And why the hell are you asking me such a dumb question?"

"Did it ever occur to you that this Garfield person or whoever it was had a gun and nearly killed one of us and that he would likely kill anyone who tried to take those coins away from him?"

"Yes."

"Did it ever occur to you that I don't want to see you shot?"

"I suppose so. Did it ever occur to you that I might want to get a pile of money so I can get out of that tunnel and that my chances of getting killed down there are pretty good too?"

"Did it ever occur to you to just leave the tunnel and do something else?"

"Like what?"

"Like anything you want to. You're bright. You're

young. You've been around. Do you realize that you're only in your twenties and you're acting like those coins are the only chance you have in life?"

"They're a very special chance," I said. "The best one I'll ever get."

She shook her head impatiently. "You'd have stayed in that tunnel forever if they hadn't come along."

"What's wrong with that?" I felt she was pushing me toward something. I didn't know what.

"Nothing, as far as I'm concerned. *You're* the one who wants out."

"It's not easy to get out."

"Hog. Don't you know you can do anything you want?"

Her words and the look on her face brought me up sharply. "That's easy for you to say, you're in another world. You don't know what it's like." I was feeling sorry for myself and annoyed that we were reading Loren's play instead of hunting for the coins. She didn't seem to understand what they meant to me. "You've made it," I said. "I haven't."

Jeannie flared. "Don't give me that. I worked my ass off in this city. It took years before I got on my feet. You're afraid to change. You're scared you'll lose."

Stung deeply, I tried to hurt back. "Did you say worked or sold?" I regretted it instantly, but the words were out, rising between us like a careless child's balloon.

Her face whitened. "Get out of my house."

My stomach clutched painfully. "I'm sorry," I mumbled. "I didn't mean that. It was a lousy thing to say."

"Get out." She meant it. I got my coat from the closet. She remained rigid on the couch, staring at the floor.

"Uh," I said, "I'll see you."

I opened the door and she stood. I turned toward her, hopefully. Her eyes glistened and she struggled to control her voice. "I never sold anything. *Never.*"

"I know. I'm sorry. I didn't mean it."

"You thought it."

"I didn't."

"I waited on tables. I checked coats. I drove a cab. I lived in a tenement. I never gave in."

"I know."

"You don't know. Go away, Hog."

I went away, back to my rooming house where I lay on the bed and stared at the ceiling and wondered how stupid and insensitive I could be and how much more I'd lose in the remaining hour and ten minutes of the worst day of my life.

I started to get up to heat some water for coffee on my hot plate, but I stopped because the way the luck was running, the thing would probably short out and burn the building down. So I remained prone and made up a couple of lists. The first was short and depressing. The second, long and mysterious.

Jeannie was on top of List One. She was followed by Rifkins and Kosinski. I assumed Burke was on also, but I hadn't seen him since he disappeared into GIRLS GIRLS GIRLS. Harry Holtzman was tentatively on as well. They were all the people who were mad at me.

After some more thought, I decided that the Metropolitan Tunnel Company deserved a spot, seeing as how I was largely responsible for starting the strike that shut down the Long Island Railroad Tunnel. I supposed the Long Island Railroad was on the list, too, but I didn't care. In fact, the only one on List One I cared about was

Jeannie. But just to be morbid I added Jones, Ericsson and Gink, whom I'd dragged all the way back to Manhattan on a fruitless towing mission. List One turned out to be longer than I'd anticipated.

I dropped it in favor of List Two, thinking that if I could figure it out, most of the people on List One might change their opinion of me. Except Jeannie. I didn't know how I would get her back.

Sean Garfield was on top of List Two. In fact, for a long time he was the only name that made any sense. List Two was my who-has-the-coins list, and the only reason I tried to add more names was that Garfield was so obviously the prime suspect it seemed advisable to look a little deeper to avoid missing the truth. I considered who else could have known the coins were at Waterside. Ericsson, Jones and Gink knew something was there. So did Burke, Kosinski and Rifkins. So did Jeannie. But she and the sandhogs were all there when the man with the gun made his move.

I tried to recall who else knew. Harry Holtzman knew we had found something because Rifkins and I had as much as told him when we gave him the coins on consignment. Reese knew something was up, but he couldn't know what. And Archibald Byron also suspected we had found something. I toyed with the notion that Byron or Reese or Holtzman could have followed me to Waterside.

I started with Reese, tracing my steps since I'd last seen him the night of the strike. Even if he had followed us while we raced down the F.D.R. in Jeannie's car, he would have found nothing. And if by some stretch of the imagination he had followed me the next day, he would have lost me when I got onto *Sadie Brown.* Of course, had he been very clever, and figured out the way we sent the gold out of the heading, he too could have learned where the barge of mud was taken. It didn't seem too likely. I dropped Reese, tentatively.

Harry Holtzman had had a much better chance. He could have waited outside his bank and followed Rifkins and me to the truck rental place and from there to Waterside. Certainly the orange truck would have been easy to trail. I tried to picture Harry doing all that. All I knew was I couldn't be sure it was beyond him. He remained on the list.

Ericsson, Jones and Gink. They knew exactly where the coins were, though they didn't know they were coins. But why didn't they go back the night they dropped me off? Being scavengers, it seemed the more likely move for them. Still, they did know something was there. I left them on the list.

That left Archibald Byron, who was as far removed from the location of the coins as Reese. In fact, the only things that made him suspect at all were the fact that he knew about the coins, and the funny business with the lawyers. I would have to check him out with the museum. Until then, he remained on the list.

I stopped list-making and reconstructed the actual robbery. The gunman was tall, medium build, and seemed scared. His gun had trembled, which led me to believe he had to be an amateur. His fear or nervousness came from more than Howard's threatening appearance, because it seemed to me that if a pro had felt threatened by Howard he would have plugged him in his tracks, no questions asked. This guy had practically pleaded for us to hold Howard back, which meant he was either not the plugging type, or feared he would miss.

Who on the list fit that description?

That narrowed things down rather quickly. Harry Holtzman was too short. Reese was too fat. Jones was black and the gunman was white. Gink was tiny.

Ericsson was about the right size. I tried to remember the man's hands, whether they were work-beaten like Ericsson's. I hadn't noticed.

Archibald Byron was the right size. Exactly. But if it had been him, he'd disguised his voice, because the gunman didn't have a British accent.

And Garfield was the right size. Again, exactly. And that was upsetting because the most likely suspect was Garfield, and he had disappeared.

The clock said twelve-thirty, which meant the worst day of my life was over, so I decided to risk making some coffee.

While I sipped it I thought of another possibility. An accomplice. The gunman could have been working in partnership with any one of the people on the List. If that were the case, then I was right back to Garfield, Holtzman, Reese, Byron, Rifkins, Kosinski, Burke, Ericsson, Jones, Gink and even, bless her, Jeannie. That was a very depressing notion, but eventually I put it out of my mind because such an accomplice would have had to be very trustworthy, otherwise he could have skipped with the coins himself. That certainly eliminated all of us who were holding our hands in the air.

I went back to my three best suspects. Tomorrow, I'd call Ericsson, check out Byron at the museum and try to get a line on Garfield.

Chapter 21

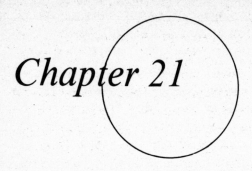

I called the job first thing in the morning. A union guy informed me that the strike was still on. The building trades unions were considering joining us. He suggested I get over to Welfare Island for some picket duty. I said I'd try and hung up.

I left the rooming house and tried to do in the cold, grey morning the things I'd planned the night before.

I started with breakfast in a diner on Queens Boulevard. Then I called the number of the Sadie Brown Towing and Salvage Enterprises, Ltd., Inc. A woman answered and said Ericsson was out in the river. She asked me to leave a number which she would relay to him by radio, but I said I didn't have a steady number and asked her if she could say I wanted to see him and could he name a time and place. She said she would and I said I'd call back in the afternoon.

Next I called Harry Holtzman on the off-chance he'd heard from Sean Garfield. He hadn't, so I caught a bus over the bridge and took the Lex up to Eighty-sixth Street and walked across town to the Metropolitan Museum of Art, the outfit Archibald Byron claimed to represent.

It was a rather grand old building, marred somewhat by very modern-looking displays around the entrance advertising special events inside. I wandered around for a little while, taking in the feel of the high-ceilinged rooms and getting briefly involved in some fantastic armor. Finally, I located the coin rooms, where I prowled around until I found Spanish gold like mine. Highly polished, and scattered on blue velvet, they looked more like trinkets than money. I think it was the crude shapes that made them seem that way. I remembered what Harry had said about the minting process being a way of certifying the weight and purity of a lump of gold.

I was wasting time so I found a guard and asked him if he knew anybody called Archibald Byron. He said of course and told me that Byron was the chief numismatist of the museum. I asked to see him, and the guard took me to an office nearby.

I asked the secretary if I could see Byron.

She smiled. "Whom shall I say is calling?"

I said the first name that came into my head. "Frederick Jones." Why? I don't know why, but Frederick Jones it was, because I didn't want my name mixed up with the company if Byron ever got back in touch with them. I'd feel pretty silly if Byron recognized me, though I hoped he wouldn't because when he had last seen me I was covered with mud and wearing my work clothes.

As soon as I saw him, I knew he'd never recognize me. He wasn't the same Archibald Byron who'd been in the hoghouse that night. He was a round, little guy in his fifties, wearing a grey sharkskin and looking exactly like a banker.

He greeted me with a puzzled smile. "Mr. Jones?"

"Thank you for seeing me, sir. I'm trying to clear up a little mix-up."

"Oh. You're from the police?"

"No." Police. Christ, what had happened? I fought the impulse to run out of his office. "No, sir. I'm from the Metropolitan Tunnel Company."

"Oh, yes. Have you found your imposter?"

"No, sir."

"Well, I've told you people all I know."

"I realize that, sir. I've just been put on the case. I wonder if you could fill me in."

"There's nothing to fill in, Mr. Jones. Apparently someone gained access to your installation by claiming to be me. I knew nothing of this until a Mr. ... Mr. somebody or other called from your company. And a little while later a man called Carson who said he was president of some blasters organization, whatever that is."

"Miners, Drillers and Blasters, Local One Forty-seven."

"Something like that. He did sound like a trade unionist."

"Have you any idea why anyone would pretend to be you, Mr. Byron?"

"None." He pressed his fingers to his temples and looked thoughtful. "Well, I shouldn't say that. If someone wished to sell some coins, it might be to his advantage to present himself as me. But not to any knowledgeable numismatist. I mean, everyone knows who I am—in my field, of course." He smiled humbly.

"Well, do you know anyone who has tried that before?"

"No one has, to my knowledge." He extracted a gold pocket watch and made a show of opening it.

"And you can think of nothing else that might help me in our investigation?"

"Nothing, Mr. Jones."

"Well, thank you, sir."

"If you do happen to apprehend this man, I'd appreciate it if you would tell me."

I promised I would and left the museum more confused than before. Whoever passed himself off as Archibald Byron had gone to the trouble of inventing the proper name, though it could have backfired on him if the company really checked. Of course, he'd come at night, after the museum was closed, and I had the feeling that Reese or whoever called just asked if the guy worked there.

It was very confusing. I should have been depressed, but I felt sort of proud of myself. I'd passed myself off as Frederick Jones of the tunnel company and Byron, the real Byron, had bought the story. I felt very free. It was exhilarating. I thought I could float around New York convincing people I was all kinds of things. Hi, I'm the Mayor. I'm Frederick Jones. I'm ... I'm ... I'm Dick Creegan and I'm looking for my coins. I found a phone booth and called Sadie Brown Towing and Salvage.

The lady said Ericsson was still on the boat but that I might catch them at Pier Fourteen. She told me it was on the East River just below the South Street Seaport

Museum. I thanked her and screwed up my courage enough to phone Jeannie. The machine said she was out so I told it I was sorry and I loved her very much. Then I walked back to Lexington Avenue and caught the train down to Wall Street and walked across to Pier Fourteen, where I found a couple of huge inflated buildings that housed a tennis club.

Negotiating my way around the gate, I walked out along the edge of the pier. The *Wavertree,* a partially restored three-masted sailing ship, floated at the museum's pier. And at the end of Fourteen I found *Sadie Brown* puffing black smoke and tugging desperately at one of the tennis club's cleats. Jones was just signaling Ericsson to up the power when he caught sight of me.

"If it ain't the cat with the secret mudpile."

I grinned and said hello.

"Want something towed?"

"You look busy."

"Never too busy to tow. Did you find what you were looking for?"

"Yes and no."

"What the hell is that supposed to mean?"

I watched his face carefully. "It means I found it and then I lost it."

Jones stared a moment. "Your name's Creegan, right?"

"Right."

"Will you tell me something, Creegan?"

"What?"

"Don't you ever come out and say what you're talking about? You're a pile of riddles, man. Now what happened?"

"What happened," I said, "was I found it and then someone came along and took it away."

Jones looked exasperated. "Found what?"

"What I was looking for."

"Which was?"

"I'd rather not say."

"So what are you doing here?"

"I want to talk to Ericsson."

"Well, you just come aboard and talk to your heart's content. Just wait a second until this thing comes loose." He yelled over his shoulder, "Pour it on, Gink." *Sadie Brown* belched smoke. The cleat creaked. Then the rope broke, whipping a piece by my head like a rifle shot. I threw myself down and sideways, too late to have saved myself if the rope had come directly at me. *Sadie Brown* went skittering across the open water, nearly smashing into the next pier. Then Ericsson got her under control and she nosed contritely back toward me.

Jones looked shaken. "That almost did you in."

"Almost." My hands were shaking.

"That's one son-of-a-bitching strong cleat is all I can say."

"Can I come on board now?"

"Sure."

I scrambled on and, while Jones eyed the pier for a more likely salvage candidate, I climbed the ladder to the wheel house and said hello to Ericsson. He seemed distant. I waited until he'd run the tug to the next cleat. Then while Jones wrapped a new line around it, Ericsson spoke. "I heard what you said to Jones."

"Good. I wanted to say it to you."

"You're making a mistake." He spoke coldly.

173

"How so?"

"You think we had something to do with it."

"I didn't say that."

"Did you just happen to be walking along this pier?"

"No," I admitted. "I was looking for you. The woman in your office told me you were here."

"That's an answering service. We don't have an office."

"I wanted to talk to you."

"We didn't take your stuff, whatever it was."

"I didn't think so, but I have to check out every possibility."

"Well, check this out. Gink replaced a piston yesterday while Travis and me drove a truckload of stuff out to Long Island."

"How did you know I lost it yesterday?"

Ericsson whirled on me, angry. For a second I thought he would swing, but he swallowed deeply and replaced his hands on the wheel. He spoke with conviction. "I don't like you, Creegan."

I started to apologize but he snapped, "Shut up. Now get this straight. I *guessed* it was yesterday because when we dropped you off at your mudpile the day before it was nearly dark and I reasoned that you had to wait for daylight to make your search. Now, I don't know what you lost and I don't care. In fact I'm sick of hearing about it. Before you get off my boat I'll tell you that you can call the Weeks boat yard in Patchogue, area code five-one-six, find the number yourself, and they'll tell you that Travis and I were there yesterday. Then go out to Gravesend and find our dock and someone there can tell you that Gink was working on the boat."

"I'm sorry," I said lamely.

"I'm not through talking," snarled Ericsson. "Because I want to tell you one more thing. And that is I am captain of this tugboat. I like being captain of this tugboat. It is what I do. What I do not do is steal things or take things that aren't mine." He raised a hand. "Except, and this is a very special except, pieces of this falling-down waterfront that nobody wants anyhow. But I don't take anything that belongs to anyone else. And that includes your secret something or other in the mud."

I moved Ericsson back to List One.

Chapter 22

I didn't like the idea of List One getting bigger, so I called Jeannie to take another stab at pruning it of its number one occupant. The answering machine came on and I told it essentially what I'd told it before. Just as I was finishing my message Jeannie picked up the phone.

"Don't hang up," she said.

"I won't if you won't."

"I'm glad you called, Hog. I have to go away and I wanted to ask you a favor."

Relieved that she hadn't mentioned our fight, I asked, "Where and what?"

Her voice was neither bubbling with love nor hostile. "Los Angeles. They want a screen test for the series."

"Congratulations."

"We'll see."

"What's the favor?"

"Could you stay at my place for a few days and watch Howard?"

I wondered why she hadn't asked Loren, but I kept my big mouth shut.

"Can you?" she asked after a moment's silence.

"Sure. Glad to."

"I really appreciate that, Hog."

"No problem," I said, meaning it. "Your place is a lot more comfortable than my place. When are you leaving?"

She groaned. "I have a seven-in-the-morning flight, tomorrow."

As casually as I could I asked, "Would you like me to drop by tonight?"

"I haven't even packed yet and I have to do a laundry and everything and try to get some sleep."

"Maybe I better not."

"I'll be back in a few days. Still have your keys?"

I felt in my pocket. They were there along with my remaining coin. "Yes."

"I thought you might have thrown them away," she said lightly.

"Not likely."

"Good . . . Listen. I'll leave my number out there by the phone. If Loren calls, would you give it to him?"

"Anything else?" I didn't want to fight, but I couldn't keep my voice neutral.

"Dammit, Hog. It's very important that he reach me. I have to know what's happening with his play. Now will you please stop acting the jealous swain?"

"Consider me stopped."

"Thank you. I'm sorry, baby, I'm all excited about this

series and upset about deciding whether to leave New York."

"I understand."

"Do you?—Hey, how'd you do today?"

"I found out who didn't take them."

"Who did?"

"I don't know."

"Hang in there, baby."

"I intend to."

"Well. Thank you for watching the place. Howard thanks you too. There's plenty of food for him. And you, too."

"You sure you don't want me to come over tonight?"

"I'm sorry, Dick. I just have so much to do."

I told her to have a good trip and wished her luck and said goodby. I wasn't thrilled with her reluctance to have me over for the night, but at least we were talking again. In the darker corners of the back of my mind I was wondering if she was being friendly so I'd watch Howard. It didn't seem her style, but the idea lingered.

I passed a newsstand and noticed the night owl edition of the *Daily News* bannered the headline "BUILDING TRADES NEXT?" Beneath it was a picture of Carson stepping into his Cadillac that was captioned "Sandhog chief to parley with building trades officials."

If anyone ever figured out what had happened, List One would be the size of the Manhattan Directory. At the moment I didn't much care.

I wandered the nearly empty streets of the financial district and tried to put together what I'd learned that day. In a way I'd accomplished a lot, having eliminated two possibilities of who had taken my coins. But knowing who hadn't was frustrating at best, because it left me right back against the wall that said Garfield in big black letters. The Archibald Byron imposter was puzzling, but no matter which way I turned that around it didn't make sense.

Feeling out of ideas, lonely, cold and rather tired and generally unhappy, I decided to head back to the rooming house for the night. I didn't like it there, but at least I could shut my door, lie down on the bed, pull the covers over my head and stop running around in circles.

I took the subway uptown and at Fifty-ninth Street caught the RR, which took me to Queensborough Plaza. There I treated myself to a cab, an expense which reminded me that, picketing aside, I had to get over to the job in the morning and pick up my last paycheck.

A stretched Lincoln limousine occupied most of the curb in front of my rooming house. Its idling engine puffed white exhaust clouds. I paid the cab driver, and as I passed the big car a homeward-bound cleaning man with a lunch pail under his arm stared at it, caught my eye and shrugged miserably. I shrugged back and climbed up the front steps.

"Mr. Creegan?"

I turned back. A uniformed chauffeur, hat in hand, hurried up to me. "Sir?"

"Talking to me?"

"Mr. Creegan?"

"Yeah?"

"Mr. Doorman would like very much to talk with you."

"Who?"

"He's in the car, sir. Could you spare a moment?"

"Doorman?" The only Doorman I knew was the guy who owned the Metropolitan Tunnel Company, and I didn't know him at all.

"Yes, sir. He's been waiting for you. If you could just

step this way." He indicated a path to the car and something in the gracious sweep of his arm implied that a plush red carpet led straight to the rear door.

"Sure," I said doubtfully. "Yeah. Glad to."

The windows were a kind of blackened glass and I couldn't see in. The chauffeur opened the door, letting escape a puff of warm air tinged with expensive tobacco smoke and more expensive perfume. I ducked down and climbed into a brightly lit compartment about the size of a small sitting room. Doorman lounged in a deep leather seat, facing front.

"I think you'll be comfortable there," he said smoothly, pointing at a similar seat facing back. I sat.

He was wearing a black tux with a violet ruffled shirt. Gold glittered on his cuffs and fingers. What hair he had was combed carefully over his shiny dome.

A remarkably beautiful woman lounged next to him with the nonchalance of a cherished mistress. Her skin was fair and stretched tautly over a fine bone structure, and were it not for her white hair she might have passed for thirty-five. She looked like a former call girl who had lucked out of the business in the nick of time. She gave me a cool look and carefully rearranged her pants-suited long legs.

Doorman opened a rosewood box that sat between us. It was a small bar with crystal glasses and decanters. "How about something to warm you up?" he asked heartily. I said thank you because it seemed easier and more polite than no.

He poured some Scotch without asking what I wanted and passed me the glass. I sipped a little off the top. It was very good.

"Perhaps you're wondering why I'm here," said Doorman.

Take away the car and the chauffeur and the beautiful woman and the crystal bar and the gold cuff links and Doorman was an oily son of a bitch. I'd seen him at the ground-breaking ceremonies and in the hoghouse the night of the blow and I hadn't liked him. Up close, putting on his superpolite front, I liked him less. The booze was giving me a headache. The white-haired woman granted me a mildly contemptuous gaze.

"I guess you want to talk to me about something."

"Correct, Mr. Creegan. As you know, we have a little problem at the tunnel."

"A strike."

"Correct." His eyes twinkled warmly and he chuckled as if to include me in hearty good-fellowship of a labor-management dispute. Then he grew serious, or, rather, deliberately replaced good humor with the look of a responsible man. Again I had the feeling I was being asked to join in. He pressed his fingers together and sighted me over them. "I've been doing some investigating and I have discovered what caused this strike."

I nodded. There was nothing I could say that wouldn't make things worse.

"And I, the company, I and we are more than prepared to settle this matter." He glanced sharply across the bar. I met his eye. Doorman smiled. I began to wonder why he was going out of his way to be so friendly. Suddenly, with no apparent signal from Doorman, the car was moving.

"Where are we going?" I asked.

"Just a little ride."

An icy tingle played across my neck until I convinced myself that building company owners don't bring their girl friends along on the nights they dump troublesome employees into Sheepshead Bay.

Doorman ceremoniously cleared his throat and got down to business. "I know what happened the other night. I know that Mr. Reese stepped out of line. I know that Mr. Kosinski and Mr. Burke and you quite rightfully refused to do his unwarranted bidding. I know that Mr. Kavanaugh came, correctly, to your aid—though," he chuckled warmly, "just between you and me, Mr. Creegan, Mr. Kavanaugh was perhaps a trifle over-zealous. Ha. Ha."

I raised my eyebrows and Doorman paled. "Not that he didn't have the right," he said hurriedly. "Of course he had the right. A fine old gentleman with a magnificent record of labor relations. He's done well for you people. I truly admire him. Yes I do."

I permitted my eyebrows to resume their customary position. Doorman relaxed. "Now," he said. "Oh. Let me fill your glass. I insist. There you are. Good. What? Oh yes, ha ha. Cheers." He tipped his glass back and licked a drop or two from the edge. "Yes. Cheers. Now. I and the company are very, very sorry this happened. Very sorry. It doesn't make us happy to see our sandhogs unhappy. Not at all. We want to apologize."

For the first time, he faltered.

"Apologize" had oozed from his mouth like the dregs of an empty toothpaste tube.

"That's very nice of you," I said. "But you'll have to talk to Burke and Kosinski and Kavanaugh. I can't speak for them."

Hate danced around the corners of his eyes and they

reflected a little skirmish while the twinkles regained control.

"Of course. Actually, you're the last, Mr. Creegan. We've already seen Mr. Kosinski. Mr. Burke has tendered his resignation. And Mr.—"

"Burke what?" I asked, sitting forward.

Doorman snapped his fingers. The white-haired woman riffled through some papers and handed him one. "Ah. Yes. Apparently he has left our employ. But he's welcome back anytime. So don't worry about Mr. Burke."

I was very worried about Mr. Burke. "Why'd he quit?" I asked.

Doorman glanced at the paper. "I don't know. Apparently he phoned for his paycheck and said he was quitting. I should assume he joined another project before it too had joined this insane dispute. Not that it's not legitimate," he added hastily.

I hardly heard him because I was trying to digest the meaning of Burke leaving the job.

"Well, Mr. Creegan?"

"Well what."

"Do you accept our a—terms?"

"Sounds fine with me."

I didn't care. I wasn't going back to work anyhow, and there was no sense in keeping half of New York off the job.

"Wonderful. Grand. You've been most magnanimous."

"My pleasure. Would you drop me back at my place now, please?"

"Could I trouble you for one last favor?"

"What?"

"We are on our way to Welfare Island." He lowered the window and peered out at the night. "In fact we've almost arrived. Would you be so kind as to tell Mr. Kavanaugh that our terms are acceptable to you?"

"You mean the apology?"

Doorman gagged on his "yes."

"O.K."

"My driver will wait to take you home."

"Good."

"Ah," said Doorman. "We're here. Now I'll go into my office. Mr. Kavanaugh and Mr. Kosinski are in your hoghouse. Just phone over the result." He leaned forward and extended his pink, soft hand. I took it. He clasped quickly, then followed the white-haired woman through the door the chauffeur held open. Perversely, I waited for the guy to come around to my side and do my door. I thanked him and walked to the hoghouse.

Rifkins was shivering by the door.

"Hi," I said. "How've you been?"

"Lousy. I'm freezing."

"Why don't you go inside?"

"Kavanaugh won't let me. Says I'm a capitalist lackey."

"So go over to the office."

He gave me a pained look. "I'd rather wait here."

"What happened to Burke?"

"He quit."

"I know. Where'd he go?"

"I haven't seen him since he went in that massage joint."

"I wonder if he found the coins."

Rifkins shrugged.

"I've been hunting all over for them," I said.

"Do me a favor, Creegan. Don't talk about coins."

"Don't you want them?"

"I want to get back to work. I want to earn a living. I'm sorry we ever found them and I'm sorrier we listened to your cockamamie ideas. We've knocked out this job, four other tunnels and, if it ain't ended soon, a couple of hundred buildings. A thousand sandhogs are freezing their butts off on picket lines. On top of that you almost got us shot. I'm sick of your coins."

"What if I find them? Then will you be sick of them or will you want your cut?"

Rifkins stared at me like I was trying to sell him scented hand lotion. "You keep 'em."

"Thanks. I just might do that."

"Do that. Kosinski's got something for you. He's inside."

"What?"

"You'll like it."

I nodded and went in. Kavanaugh motioned me over to join him and Kosinski. "Over here, lad. Did they give you a hard time?"

"They gave me two drinks and drove me here in a limousine."

"Swine."

"It wasn't that bad."

"What did they say?"

"They want to apologize."

"That's what they told Kosinski. Do you accept?"

"Sure."

Kavanaugh looked mildly disappointed. "Well, then that's it. We've won, boys. Not a big fight. But every one counts. You should be proud you were in the forefront." He wrinkled his brow. "Though I noticed, Brother Creegan, you were absent from the picket line."

I bowed my head. "I was and I'm sorry. I was very busy."

"Next time," said Kavanaugh. I didn't bother to tell him there wouldn't be a next time for me. He smiled sadly around the empty hoghouse, savoring the last moments of his strike. Then he struggled to his feet and shuffled across the room to the phone. Kosinski and I looked at each other.

"Why'd Burke quit?" I asked.

"I don't know."

"Do you think he found the coins?"

"No."

"Do you mean because if he had he would have told us?"

"No. He wouldn't tell us."

"Then why do you think he didn't find them?"

"You didn't find them. They can't be found. The guy who held us up is gone. There is no way to find him. He got in a truck and drove away and he could be anyplace now and we'll never know. Pretty soon he'll sell them and then it's all over."

"I'll find him."

"Good luck. Here. This'll help." He handed me an envelope.

"What's this?"

"Seven hundred and forty-eight dollars. Me and Rifkins got those coins back from that dealer who lent you the money. We sold them to another dealer. That's your cut."

I looked inside. "Thanks."

"If you see Burke, tell him I got the same for him."

"Did you sell your second coin?"

"My second coin was a piece of lead. Rifkins's was good. We'll sell that and split."

"I wonder what mine is worth?"

"Didn't you look at it?"

"I've been running around for three days."

"Check it out. Maybe it's a good one."

"What are you going to do?" I asked.

"Go back to work."

"What about the coins?"

"I've done O.K. I got the seven hundred and forty-eight and I'll get some more from the other coin."

"What about your farm?"

"I'll get it one of these days."

"I'm getting the coins."

"Good luck."

"I'll see you around," I said. I waved goodby to Kavanaugh, who sat moodily by the phone, went out, nodded to Rifkins and told him I thought he could go in now. Then I walked over to the office and tried to get my last paycheck. They wouldn't give it to me, so I barged into the inner office to find Doorman. He wasn't there.

I talked somebody into mailing the check to me and went out to my limousine. It was gone, so I went back inside and called a cab which eventually came and drove me back to Long Island City, where I crawled into bed and fell asleep wondering what the hell I would do in the morning.

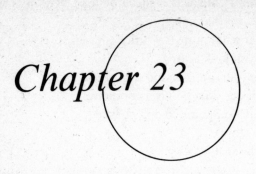

Chapter 23

I went to Jeannie's apartment the next morning to feed and walk Howard. I opened the door apprehensively, not sure how seriously he took his home-guarding duties, but he greeted me like a long lost friend, licking my hand and bounding off the furniture like a two-hundred-pound rubber ball.

"How you doing?" I asked.

He rolled over on his back and seemed to swoon with delight.

"Lonely already?" I asked. "She's only been gone a few hours." He stood up, felling an end table. I righted it and asked him if he wanted to go for a walk. He hurled himself against the door, which I took to mean yes, so I attached his leash and took him down to the street.

I thought we might head up Sixth Avenue and buy a newspaper, but Howard strained westward, so we went westward along Bedford Street, then over to St. Luke's Park to terrorize a gang of German shepherds and on toward the river until we reached the Morton Street Pier where I'd met the good ship *Sadie Brown*. Howard tugged me all the way out to the end and flopped down for a rest. I took a nearby bench and started my first serious thinking of the day.

It seemed I'd been living with the missing coins for a long, long time, but as I went through all that had happened, I realized it had only been a week since I'd found the first two in the heading. I pulled out the one I had left and commenced to idly scrape the mud with Jeannie's keys. It had had time to dry hard and the flakes clung stubbornly.

I scraped and picked and wondered what Burke had done. It was entirely possible that he had just plain quit the job. As far as I knew he wasn't married and there was nothing to stop him from moving on when he felt so inclined. Still, the timing was odd and I couldn't ignore it. The trouble was, it didn't seem to make much difference whether I ignored it or not. No matter what I did, it didn't bring me closer to the coins.

Neither was I making much headway with the rock-hard mud on the coin. The keys weren't sharp enough so I dropped them back in my pocket. I'd resume scraping with a knife in Jeannie's kitchen. I missed her so much. With the money Kosinski gave me, and whatever I might clear with the coin in my pocket, plus the twenty-five hundred or so I could get for the first two, I'd have enough to go to Los Angeles. Now that she was gone, I knew I had to follow her out if she stayed. I didn't know if it would work out, but if I could find something to do there, we might be able to take up where we'd left off.

She had been right about me. There was no reason why I couldn't try something new. I didn't know what, but that really opened the possibilities. A lot of other people had gone to California and found something.

A seagull swooped past Howard's nose, rousing him from his stupor. He stood up and stretched and jerked the leash, which meant I was supposed to go home with him.

I bought a couple of cheeseburgers on the way back for lunch, and while I was opening a few cans of food for Howard he ripped open the bag and ate one of the cheeseburgers. I called him a son of a bitch and he snarled and went for the second cheeseburger. Foolishly I reached to stop him. He didn't snap at me, but he gave a look that said he was considering the idea. I hesitated, wondering how big an issue I wanted to make of the incident, when the phone rang.

I went for it, grateful for the opportunity to save face and hand, but it stopped after one ring. I shrugged and turned away, but a moment later an excited voice filled the room. I spun around looking for the source before I realized Jeannie had left the answering machine on the monitor position, something she often did when she wanted to see who was calling before she picked up.

"Jeannie," the voice yelled. "I got the backers. *Nassau Tragedy* goes into rehearsal next week."

Loren. Son of a bitch Loren, my arch-rival.

"Jeannie, if you're there please answer. We're on. You're on. The lead is yours. They loved you." He waited a few seconds. "Call me as soon as you can," he said. "Isn't it fantastic?" He hung up.

I stood still, my mind racing, wondering what to do. Loren sounded very happy. Apparently he didn't know

Jeannie had gone out for the television test. I felt a very strong temptation to forget the whole thing and maybe even erase the tape. Jeannie could stay in Los Angeles. Loren could produce his play with a different lead. I could go to Los Angeles and be with Jeannie, and everyone, including me, would be happy.

I approached the answering machine and began to inspect it to figure out how to erase the tape. I told myself that Jeannie had a better future in Hollywood. I told myself Loren's play was lousy and would bomb the first night and that I was protecting Jeannie from ruining her career in it. I even told myself that it wouldn't be good for Loren to be so closely involved with his leading lady at a time when he should be devoting all of his energies to producing his play.

Then I told myself I would be the lowest bastard in New York City if I didn't call Loren and give him Jeannie's Los Angeles number.

I found her personal phone book and Loren's number, which wasn't easy because I didn't know his last name, which turned out to be Fone, of all things, and I called him. And I'll even admit that when his phone rang I nearly hung up.

He answered in a voice that sounded a little less electronic than the one I had just heard. I was able to make out a slight lisp on certain words.

"This is Dick Creegan."

His brief silence tipped me off to something I had never considered. He was very likely as upset by my friendship with Jeannie as I was with his.

"Hello. Um. How are you?"

I said, "I heard your call a moment ago and I have to tell you something."

"Where's Jeannie?" he asked.

"Los Angeles."

"WHAT?"

"Los Angeles."

"WHY?"

"She's taking a screen test for a TV series."

"OH NO."

"I'm afraid so," I said.

"She didn't tell me she was going anywhere," he wailed.

"It happened suddenly," I said sympathetically. I could have added that I only learned at the last minute, but there was a limit to how nice a guy I was going to be.

"This is simply awful." His voice rose in pitch and the lisp grew more pronounced. "I must talk to her."

"That's why I called," I said more casually than I felt. "She left her number out there for you."

"What is it?"

"213-344-5666."

"Say it again. I better write it down." He sounded a little relieved. I said it again. He read it back correctly.

"Thank you. Thank you. Thank you," he said.

"That's O.K. She asked me to give it to you." I bit my tongue. He didn't have to know that.

"I'll call her right away."

"I doubt she's there yet. She had a seven A.M. flight."

"I'll leave a message."

"Great idea. Congratulations on getting backers. I hope you do all right with your play."

"Could I ask you something?" he said.

"What?" I was starting to wish the conversation was over. I'd about reached my limit of nice-guyness for the afternoon.

"Do you always talk like that?"

"What do you mean?"

"You sound very much like you sounded on that tape you did with Jeannie. I was wondering where you learned voice."

"I didn't learn voice. I just talk like this."

"Oh. Well, you certainly sound like you learned somewhere."

There followed a silence and I thought one of us should say goodby. Before I could, though, he asked, "Honestly, what did you think of that scene you read?"

"Honestly? I thought it was awful."

"I've rewritten it. I knew it was awful and as soon as I heard you and Jeannie run through it I knew what was wrong."

I was curious. "What was wrong?"

"Well, tell me. You said it was awful. Why?"

"Because two people married for seventeen years don't talk like they met yesterday."

"I'm glad you said that. I thought the same thing."

I wondered how the hell Loren and I were discussing his play like old friends when we were supposed to be rivals for the leading lady.

Loren said, "When I figured it out, thanks to your tape, I nearly died. I thought, my God, the entire thing has to be done over."

"Does it?"

"No. I'm fairly certain it's fine. You know, I did that scene when I'd been pushing myself too fast. I was tired and rushing and I just lost the characters. But I think they sound all right in the rest of it. God, I hope so."

"You'd know by now," I said.

"Would you like to read the rest of it and tell me what you think?"

"I don't know much about plays."

"You were absolutely right about that scene. Would you have the time to give the rest of it a read? It would make me feel a lot better."

"I have time," I said, flattered that a guy who could write a play wanted to know what I thought of it.

"Thank you," he said. "How can I get it to you?"

"I'm staying at Jeannie's place."

"Oh."

"Watching Howard."

"I pity you."

"He's all right."

"Personally, I can't stand the beast. But don't tell him I said that. Listen, I'm very busy getting the theatre. Would it be all right if I sent it over by messenger?"

"Sure. I'll read it right away."

"Thank you so much."

We said goodby and I sat by the phone, pleased that I'd called him, and rather surprised by how unsure of himself he sounded. Probably because I'd always pictured him as competition, I'd built up an image of a very successful, arrogant guy. It was nice to know I wasn't the only one with doubts.

I slipped Jeannie's number under one of the phone's feet and went back to the kitchen to finish preparing Howard's lunch. Suddenly, halfway there, I spun around and leaped back at the phone. It had hit me that I'd ignored the most obvious way to locate Sean Garfield. I scrambled through Jeannie's papers until I found the Manhattan Directory. I couldn't believe how dumb I'd been, but when I'd discovered that he had abandoned his shop, I'd naturally assumed that meant he had gone to ground, as writers like Adam Hall are fond of saying.

It's amazing how a person can sabotage his own brain.

I knew he'd left the shop and, because it had been so sudden, and in conjunction with the gunman taking my coins, I told my brain he had vanished completely, never bothering to check where he lived.

Gardner ... Gardstein ... Garfinkle ... back a column ... Garfield, Richard, Samuel, Garfield and Rosen C.P.A.s. No Sean. I looked for an initial S. None.

I leaned over the book and butted my head into the page. He had to have a phone. Everyone has a phone. I scanned the column again. No Sean Garfield. Disgusted, I slammed the book shut and dropped it on the floor.

But maybe he didn't live in Manhattan. Of course. He wouldn't live in Manhattan because he wasn't the type. I remembered the neat, slicked-back hair, the white shirt, the leather pen and pencil holder. He had to live in Queens. I dialed information, asked for Sean Garfield in Queens.

592-9212. 99-05 Fifty-ninth Avenue.

The first real smile in several days grew on my face. It got wider and wider. I had the son of a bitch. He had most likely moved, but neighbors, storekeepers, bartenders and friends would know something. I'd also check out travel agents in the area in case he'd taken a trip.

I dialed the number to make sure it was the right Sean Garfield. A woman answered and my hopes sank. I said I had a coin to sell and asked if I could speak to Mr. Garfield.

"He's at the shop."

"What?"

"He's at the shop."

"*Sean* Garfield?"

"He's my boy."

I shook the receiver and looked into the little holes. "Are you *Mrs.* Garfield?"

Her voice became wary. "Who's calling, please?"

"Frederick Jones. I wanted to sell Mr. Garfield a coin. Are you his wife?"

She laughed. "He's my boy. I'm his mother."

Of course. The son of a bitch would live with his mother to save on rent. But his mother didn't seem to know he'd closed his business. "Well, I'm sorry to bother you, Mrs. Garfield, but I called your home because I'd heard Mr. Garfield had gone . . . left his business."

"Who told you that?"

"Harry Holtzman."

"Harry? You must have heard wrong. Harry's place of business is just a few doors down from ours."

"I didn't know you were in the business, Mrs. Garfield."

"Well, not much any more. I worked with my husband. The poor man is gone now and Sean runs it. What did you want to sell?"

I blurted out the first thing that came to mind that wasn't Spanish gold. "An Indian head nickel."

"Are you a collector, Mr. Jones?"

"No. I'm selling off an estate."

"I didn't think so," she said coolly. "You can find Sean at the shop. He's usually there until ten, at least. Goodby."

Chapter 24

It was late in the afternoon and dark when I got to Forty-seventh Street, and I started by checking all the stores on both sides between Sixth and Seventh Avenues on the off-chance that Garfield had moved without telling his mother. Then I went to Harry Holtzman's to see what he had to say about it, but his shop was dark and he didn't answer my pounding on the door.

Puzzled, I walked over to GIRLS GIRLS GIRLS just to make sure it was where Garfield's place had been. His old sign was still there exactly as I remembered it. Mrs. Garfield was either very confused or a practiced liar.

A couple of guys came out looking guiltily satisfied. I tried to get a look inside, but the door slammed quickly behind them. Finally, because it was so cold and because I was at my wit's end, I went in. I didn't have enough cash with me to buy a handshake, but maybe somebody could tell me where Garfield had moved.

A tiny foyer opened into a medium-sized reception room. There was a red shag rug on the floor and the walls were covered with *Playboy* centerfolds. The lights were dim by the entrance, brighter on the other side where a couple of couches sat. In front of the couches was a desk and behind the desk, turning away from me talking to a stunning Eurasian girl, was a heavy-set guy in a turtleneck who looked like the bouncer.

The girl noticed me, smiled brightly, and indicated my presence with a slight nod to the bouncer. He turned toward me, his head sort of following his shoulders. I stared for a moment, then started laughing. Once going, I couldn't stop until I had to support myself on the wall.

"What the hell's got into you?" asked Burke. I tried to answer and laughed some more. He had had his hair styled by someone who knew what he was doing. A small pinky ring glittered on his left hand. The turtleneck looked like cashmere and as he stood up and came toward me, a sheepish grin on his face, I noticed he was wearing knitted pants in a subdued hound's tooth.

I let go of the wall and looked him up and down. He glared back, trying to put up a tough front, but obviously very pleased with himself.

I said, "I'll bet you haven't left here since the other night."

"You'd win," he said. He was a different Burke. A new Burke, subdued, the truculent look gone. A man in his intended state.

"How did this happen?" I asked.

"Feel like a drink?" he asked.

"Yeah. I'm freezing."

He led me to the couch. The beautiful girl had vanished. Burke poured a couple of hefty shots of Teachers. I downed mine quickly, loving the warmth. He refilled my glass, offered me a cigar, which I declined, lighted one for himself and puffed contentedly.

"You work here?" I said.

"I'm the manager."

"How'd you get the job?"

He grinned and winked. "Remember when I came in here to check out Garfield?" I nodded. "Well, I got sort of involved and before I knew it it was closing time and I wasn't ready to leave. Garfield wanted to throw me out, but the girls talked him into letting me bed down for the night."

"*Garfield?*"

"Yeah. So the next day—"

"*Sean Garfield* the coin guy?"

"Yeah, so like I said, I stayed the night and—"

I held up my hand. "Stop. Wait. Where is he now?"

"Garfield?"

"Yes," I yelled. "Where is he?"

"I don't know. Selling coins, probably."

"Our coins?"

"He didn't take them."

"How do you know?"

"I know. He's my boss. He didn't take them."

"Are you sure?"

"Of course I'm sure. Look, kid. I checked him out right away. I asked some of the girls and they said he was here all afternoon."

"They could be covering for him."

"Not to me, kid. They're on my side."

"Burke," I said wearily. "Why didn't you tell me this?

199

I've been running all over the place trying to find him."

Burke winked again. "Listen, kid—"

"And stop calling me kid."

"Creegan, baby, I just came up for air this morning. It's been a hell of a party."

"Thanks."

"I called you this morning. The landlady said you was out. So I called the office. They said you didn't come in for work. What'd you do, quit?"

"Yeah. I think so. What about you?"

"Me?" he laughed. "Somebody else can dig holes in the ground. Not me. I got plenty right here to keep me busy."

I downed my second drink in the hopes it would clear my head. It didn't. I started to ask Burke to explain how Garfield happened to own a massage parlor, but a phone rang, seemingly near, but oddly muted.

"Hang on," said Burke. He ignored the phone on the desk, and opened a drawer which contained a second phone, red, the one that was ringing, and said, "Sean Garfield, Numismatist Extraordinaire. Oh—hello, Mrs. Garfield. No, Mr. Garfield stepped out to an auction. Yes. This is Mr. Burke. No. He didn't say when he would return. Yes. Of course. Wait. Let me write it down."

Winking again and shoving the bottle my way, Burke found a pen and paper and resumed his conversation. "Okay, Mrs. Garfield. Right. I've got it. Frederick Jones. Yes. I'll tell him. Oh, Mrs. Garfield? He did mention that he might stay in the city tonight and not to wait up for him? . . . Well, I think he feels he should stay close to his buyer while he's in town . . . Yes. I'll tell him. I'm sure he'll stay at a good hotel . . . The Royalton? I'll tell him. Goodby, Mrs. Garfield."

Burke dropped the phone back in the drawer and slid it shut.

"His old lady is driving us both nuts."

"She told me he's still in the coin business."

"He is—part-time. When'd you talk to her?"

"A little while ago. Frederick Jones."

Burke looked at the paper. "Aha. O.K. Well, Garfield's in the clear, kid. You can cross him off your list."

"What happens if Mrs. Garfield calls the other phone and you answer, 'Edwardian Delights—you want it, we do it'?"

"The red phone's the only number she's got."

I drank some more Scotch, feeling warm and woozy. "How come Garfield opened a massage parlor?" I asked.

"Money," said Burke. "It's fantastic money. He already had the location with a long-term cheap lease. Besides, he hates coins."

"But he's still doing some coin business."

"It's a good front. Keeps his mother off his back. I'm just hoping the old bag doesn't decide to come into the city one day." Burke filled my glass for what had to be the fourth or fifth time. The room was turning red and the centerfold maidens' breasts seemed to grow larger.

"Hang on a minute," said Burke. A guy had come in and was standing tentatively by the door. Burke gave him a friendly smile. "Come on in, fellow. What would you like?"

I turned away because he looked embarrassed. Burke pressed a bell and several girls pranced into the room. I concentrated on the floor until the customer had made his choice.

"Another one, kid?"

I covered my glass. "I'm falling over already."

"You look pretty bad."

"I am," I mumbled. "I don't know what to do next."

Burke nodded sympathetically. "How about something to take your mind off it?" He jerked his head toward the back rooms.

"No thanks."

"On the house. Enjoy yourself."

"No, thanks anyway."

"What's wrong with it?"

I stood, swayed, then pulled myself stiffly erect. "I'm in love."

"Suit yourself."

"Thanks for the drinks."

"What are you going to do now?"

"Get some sleep, if I can find my way home."

"Better take a cab."

"Yeah." I stumbled toward the door. "By the way," I said, "Kosinski said to tell you he has seven hundred and forty-eight bucks of yours."

Burke smiled happily. "How come?"

"He and Rifkins sold the coins we hocked to buy the metal detector. That's your cut."

"Beautiful."

"Do you have your second coin?"

His face dropped. "Yeah. A frigging screw."

"Tough break. Anyhow, you cleared the seven hundred."

Burke brightened. "Right. Hey? Did you get screwed too?"

"I haven't looked yet."

"What you waiting for?"

"I want to find the rest of them, first."

"They're gone."

"I'll find them."

"How?"

"I don't know. I'll figure it out."

"They're gone, kid. Whoever took them must of sold them by now."

"I doubt that. It'll take a while to set up the deal."

"You're wasting your time. You better get over to the job or you'll be nowhere."

The cold air braced me up enough to make me walk downtown instead of taking a cab. By the time I reached the Village I was freezing, but nearly sober. I found Jeannie's superintendent and he gave me a thick manila envelope.

Loren had attached a note asking me to please call him so he'd know the script hadn't gotten lost in transit. I put up some coffee, laid the script on the coffee table, and phoned him. He said he hoped I would enjoy the play, and mentioned that he hadn't been able to get Jeannie yet. We agreed that her flight had been fouled up.

When the coffee was ready I poured a cup and stretched out on the couch with the script. At first, as I read, I used it to keep the coins away. But very shortly, the play grabbed me hard. I pored over it, regretting each finished page and apprehensively watched the unread pile get smaller. He had completely rewritten the one scene I already knew and I thought he did it perfectly.

When it was over, I was very impressed by Loren Fone. He'd clipped a little note at the end. "I need a title. Think about it."

Chapter 25

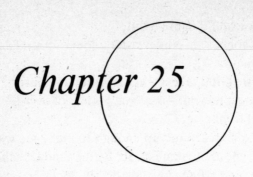

Two days later Loren and I were very worried.

Jeannie had disappeared. She hadn't called either of us, and the people who answered the number she'd left said she wasn't there. An agent had called from Los Angeles, screaming that she was blowing the whole deal and practically accusing me of hiding her whereabouts.

The airline confirmed that she had flown to L.A. Loren was calling several times a day, with theories of what had happened, all based on the fact that Jeannie tended toward sudden bouts of irrational behavior.

"I've never noticed that," I had said. It was during one of our phone conversations on the first day she was missing.

"Well, I've know her for a long time, Dick."

"Do you mean she goes crazy?"

"No. No. No. Nothing like that. It's just that every now

and then she does something unexpected and it's always surprising because, as you've probably noticed, she's the kind of person who clings to stability."

"I'm not sure I follow you."

"Look at her apartment. I don't know how many people's places you've seen around the city, but most people don't put that much care into decor. That whole place is a study in stability."

I looked around the room. He was right. Each piece looked like it had occupied its spot for a long, long time.

"That's really Jeannie," Loren continued. "More than the Jeannie who parades with Howard and drives that obscene car."

"So where is she?" I asked.

"Probably sitting in a room someplace trying to make up her mind about something."

"I hope you're right."

"So do I," he said. "I wrote that play for her, you know."

"It seemed that way."

"I couldn't bear to see anyone else do the part."

I had wondered if that was all he cared about, but when he kept calling for news and reassurance, neither of which I could give him, I realized that he cared as much for her as I did.

Finally, late in the afternoon of the second day, Loren called and asked if I minded if he came over. He said he thought we could have a discussion about his play. It sounded like he needed company, which was fine with me because I was feeling the need of company also.

He handed me a bottle of white wine when he came in. I took it in my left hand and shook his with my right. He looked about thirty-five, taller than me, but built much more slimly. His clean-shaven face was the kind you're sure you've seen before, even-featured, pleasant, almost bland. I tried to fit the face to the words in his play and were it not for the glittering intelligence in his eyes I couldn't have put the two together.

"Where's Howard?" he asked with a nervous glance.

"Sleeping in the bedroom."

"I'd feel a lot better if you'd close the door."

"I already did."

He gave me a relieved smile and walked over to the couch.

"Want to drink some of this?" I asked, holding up the bottle.

"I'd prefer coffee, if there's some around."

I put a light under the pot and sat in the chair across from him. For a few minutes there was a nervous silence. I don't know what he was thinking, but I was fighting hard not thinking about him in bed with Jeannie. I used the coffee as an excuse to leave the room and think of something to say.

When I brought it in, Loren was thumbing through his script.

"Come up with a title?" he asked.

Essentially it was a story about a seventeen-year marriage in Nassau County that ran into an attractive young English graduate student who was staying in the couple's home while taking a year at Columbia. He and the husband would commute into the city four days a week, the Englishman to school, the husband to his brokerage office. On the fifth day, the husband went into his office and the Englishman stayed home to study, until one day he fell into bed with the wife.

It sounds simple but it wasn't, and it deserved more

than the working title, *A Nassau County Tragedy*. For one thing, though not light, it was often very funny.

"How about *The Friday Exchange?*" I said tentatively.

Loren thought a moment. "I don't love it."

"Yeah. What about just, *Exchange?*"

"Sounds like one of those dreadful paperbacks about wife-swapping."

"Yeah," I agreed. I stared at the ceiling and played with the words.

Loren said, slowly, "I was thinking about something like *Friday in Nassau.*"

"Which Nassau?" I asked. "It sounds tropical."

He smiled broadly. "I know."

"Friday."

Loren stared at me. He mouthed the word and his face lit up. "I love it. I positively love it. *Friday*. Yes."

I grinned at him, very proud of myself. He repeated the title a few more times and I could see it was what he had wanted. He demanded that we celebrate and open the wine, which he did, filling a couple of glasses and toasting, *"Friday."*

Then, as the windows turned black, he talked about the play and how he'd come to New York fifteen years before and the small successes he'd had and how *Friday* was the culmination of all he had learned. Then he asked me about myself and I told him about sandhogging and kicking around the world with my old man, and he interrupted now and then to say he wished he'd had such experiences instead of coming from a very ordinary home in upstate New York.

As we talked and grew more comfortable with each other, I liked him more and more. I also came to the conclusion that while he would always be Jeannie's close friend, he would never be her lover nor had he ever been, because he was gay and seemingly happily so. He didn't say he was but his stories and the way he talked and moved as he became at ease left no doubt.

Then, noticing how interested I was whenever he mentioned Jeannie, he told me bits and pieces of what he knew of her life. I realized that they had confided in each other for years and that, while he told me the outlines of her own struggle in the theatre, he betrayed no secrets.

"You're the best thing that ever happened to her, you know that, don't you?" Loren said, breaking a comfortable silence.

"I've only known her for about three weeks."

"I know. But I know Jeannie and she's never been so happy."

"Does it matter that she's older than me?" I asked.

"No."

A key clicked in the front door. Jeannie flung it open, saw Loren and me, and blinked surprise. Her face was radiant. She threw her coat off and leaped into the room. "I'm free," she said triumphantly.

She skipped up to Loren, took his cheeks between her hands and kissed him. Then she danced to me and wrapped her arms around my shoulders and kissed me on the mouth. I kissed back.

"Where the hell have you been?" asked Loren.

A heavy thumping from the direction of the bedroom said that Howard had heard his mistress. Jeannie disappeared down the hall and Loren and I listened to them greet each other with happy squeals. She returned in a minute with Howard rubbing his nose against the back of her legs. Loren paled, but Howard was too involved with Jeannie to notice him or me.

"You scared both of us, silly," Loren said to Jeannie.

"A thousand apologies to both of you. I'm fine."

"What happened?" I asked.

Jeannie grabbed my wine glass and emptied it in a swallow. She looked at Loren and me, her smile climbing into her tremendous eyes. Then, sitting between us and draping her arms over our shoulders she said, "The minute, the *second*, I got off the plane in Los Angeles I knew I was making a mistake. The studio had a car waiting for me, but I saw it in time and caught a cab to the station."

"What station?" asked Loren.

"The *train* station. I remembered all those New York screenwriters who used to come fleeing home on the *Super Chief* and I thought that's the way to go.

"But no *Super Chief.* So I got a ticket on something called the *California Zephyr* which took me to Chicago and there I got a plane which took me to New York and then I got a cab which took me back home to my two favorite men in the world. That's what happened."

She was brimming with smiles and laughter. "The thing about taking the train is that you have a lot of time to think you made a mistake."

"Did you?" Loren asked.

"Absolutely not. I'm an actress and I live in New York. Now tell me how you two got together?"

"Dick read the play," said Loren. "And gave me a title."

"What?"

"Friday."

She cocked her head. "Not bad. Not bad at all. Now all you have to do is get it produced."

"I'm producing it myself. I got backers and plenty of money and we'll open in the fall."

"Loren," yelled Jeannie, hugging him hard and kissing

his cheek. It occurred to me that if Loren had remained gay all those years around Jeannie, he was very committed.

"Can I be the wife?" asked Jeannie, smiling.

"You know you are," Loren said gently. "Don't be coy."

"Isn't it a wonderful play, Dick?"

"I liked it a lot."

"Let Dick be the Englishman," said Jeannie.

"I can't act."

"We'll teach you. And Loren will be the husband."

"Loren might be the husband," I said. "But I'm not an actor."

"Who knows," said Loren. "Seriously, Jeannie, I've considered doing the husband, but I've written it and I'm directing and also producing and I think I'd rather get somebody different to do the husband because I need somebody around to tell me I'm going wrong." He turned to me. "It's easy to get self-indulgent when you do it all yourself," he explained.

"Well at least let Dick be the Englishman."

"I can't act."

Loren smiled. I felt Jeannie was pushing him. She said, "I'll teach you." She was so happy that I couldn't tell if she was kidding or not, but I was sure of one thing and that was that Loren's first big play didn't need an amateur.

"I can't do an English accent," I said.

"They're easy," Jeannie said. "Loren? Say something in British."

"I wouldn't know what to say," said Loren in a slightly flat British accent.

Chapter 26

"Howard," I called to the sleeping hulk. "How would you like to go for a walk with Loren and me?" At "walk" his ears pricked and he leaped up.

"Good idea," said Jeannie. "I've got to take a bath and get out of these clothes."

"Certainly," mumbled Loren. "Yes."

"Hog," said Jeannie. "Could you help me with this bag?" She pointed at the light suitcase she'd carried to and from Los Angeles and disappeared down the hall to the bedroom. I took the bag and followed her, leaving Loren looking stricken on the couch. Jeannie grabbed it and shoved it under the bed. She moved close and nibbled my lips. "I just wanted to tell you not to bring Loren back with you because I've been sleeping alone for four days since you were so mean and I can't stand it anymore."

She misread the look on my face. "He'll understand. Don't worry."

She pushed me out of the room and closed the door. I went back to the living room and attached Howard's leash. Then I took my coat and Loren's coat from the closet, put mine on and tossed him his. He looked at it like he'd never seen it.

"Let's go," I said, trying to control my voice. With a resigned shrug he put it on and went out the door.

Neither of us spoke in the elevator. Nor did we say anything in the lobby or for the first two blocks we walked up Sixth.

We had to stop for the light at Bleecker.

"How much did you get for them?" I asked.

"A hundred thousand," he said dully.

"They were worth about a million," I said.

"Seven hundred and fifty thousand, perhaps, if you sold them piecemeal over a few years. I didn't have the time. I inquired with various people. They all said the same thing."

"Who'd you sell them to?"

Loren sighed. "A nameless, faceless person who will sell them to another nameless, faceless person, who will sell them to a museum for much more than either you or I would ever get."

The light changed and we followed Howard across the street. "What did you hope to get when you came to the tunnel?"

"I knew you'd found the two coins."

"Jeannie told you?"

"No," he said sharply. He touched my shoulder. "She knew nothing about it. *Knows* nothing about it."

"I believe that. How'd you know about them?"

"You left a message on the machine."

"You listen to her messages?"

"No. I was there when she played it back. I don't think

she even knew I'd heard." Howard tugged me and Loren had to step quickly to catch up. "I know a little about coins and I thought if I were lucky I might find something valuable. Some of them run around twenty-five thousand dollars."

"How'd you happen to pick the name Archibald Byron? I found out he's real."

"I met him at a party. I remembered the name and assumed that if someone at the tunnel questioned me they could call the museum and with luck the museum would say that Archibald Byron worked there."

"Weren't you afraid I'd recognize you when you came over today?"

"You didn't. I know make-up. The weathered skin and the mustache and glasses were as good as a mask for an ordinary face like mine."

"Where's the money?"

"Some of it is in the bank. I paid out a big piece to the theatre. I got a good deal putting a lot of cash up front."

It seemed that I should have been angry, but I wasn't. I wasn't thrilled, but neither was I mad.

"I can give you some of it now and maybe if I can get another backer I can siphon some more to you."

"I don't want the backer's money."

"I'll try to get the money back from the theatre-owner."

"No."

"He'll give me some of it."

"And then *Friday* won't be produced and Jeannie won't have the job. Tell me something. I really don't know much about plays. Is it as good as I think it is?"

"Yes."

"Will it be a success?"

"Box office? Maybe. You can't count on it, though."

213

"I'll tell you what," I said. "Consider me a backer. Not for the whole thing, you did some work for it, but a part. A large part."

"Do you mean it?" Loren asked.

"Yes."

"Do you want to play the Englishman?"

"Don't be ridiculous."

He sighed. "I'm sorry about this, now. It was easy when I didn't know you."

"Tell me one more thing," I said, feeling anger mix with confusion. "Do you know how close you came to killing Jeannie?"

He laughed. I whirled at him, but he held his hands out and said, "Blanks."

"Huh?"

"A stage prop."

"It looked damned real to me."

"It was. But the cartridges were blanks."

It struck me that it took a lot of guts to try to knock over four sandhogs with an unloaded gun and I said so.

Loren laughed again. "Had I known what it would be like I would not have done it. When that big fellow went for the shovel I thought I was dead."

"You almost were."

"It was terrifying."

"You covered it pretty well." We paused by the West Fourth Street Station. "I'm going back to Jeannie's now. Don't ever tell her what happened."

"Of course not."

"I mean it. There is no reason why she has to know."

Loren grinned weakly. "What happens if it's a smash and you're suddenly rich?"

"I'll tell her I found the coins."

Chapter 27

Jeannie's bedroom door was closed. "Don't come in," she called, "I'm making myself beautiful."

"You are beautiful."

"I'll tell you when I'm beautiful. Fix yourself a drink or something."

I went back to the living room and poured some Scotch. Then I took a kitchen knife and picked the mud off my last coin. Any idea I might have had about discovering a twenty-five-thousand-dollar dated coin disappeared along with the center of the chunk of mud. The hollow, empty middle grew bigger and bigger until I believed there was nothing inside at all.

But I hit solid material around the edges. I took it into the kitchen and rinsed it under hot water. The rest of the mud washed away, revealing a delicate gold ring with a carved face on top. I buffed it gently with a dish towel until all the mud was gone and the ring gleamed.

I held it to the light. The face was intricate and looked like it belonged to a mythical animal. I studied it awhile and concluded that it looked like Howard's face.

I dropped it in my shirt pocket where it wouldn't get scratched. It would make a nice present for someone.